ADDIE

Pack of Misfits

RAVEN KENNEDY

To all the misfits.

It's okay to be different.

ADDIE

I live with a pack of misfits.

The runts and the prey. The scarred and the deformed. The albinos and, on the opposite spectrum, those with melanism. The rogues, the banished, the crazies, the rare, the small, and the weak. We're all welcome in Pack Aberrant. In a world where only quintessential predator shifters are respected, life isn't always kind to those of us who are different.

And it's not just other shifters. Even some of the other paranormal, arcane races—or Canes, as we all call ourselves—look down on us, too. The only people who don't judge us are humans, but that's just because they don't know what we are.

Most of us would probably be miserable or dead if Hugo hadn't formed this pack and taken us in. Aside from being the best alpha I've ever known, he's an albino jaguar. He knows what it's like to be unwanted.

When he was born, his pack leader declared him an aberrant. But in their pack, that title was like a contagious disease, something to be hated and avoided. All because his fur and eyes were a different color than that of his kin.

Hugo was constantly challenged by other jaguars, and he has the scars to prove it. As soon as he was old enough to apply for rogue status, he left and never looked back. He formed Pack Aberrant as a big "fuck you" to his old leader, and the misfits had been lining up at his door ever since.

Unlike other alphas who rule with fear, Hugo is loved and respected by every single member of his pack.

Our pack may not be the strongest, but we totally win the most diverse trophy. There are just over a hundred of us here in Northern California, and we're a mishmash of bizarre animals that probably look weird together, but we fit. We have each other's backs and we are fiercely loyal to our hodgepodge pack.

We have our own pocket of land in the Sierra Nevada Mountains, with plenty of space to roam. Everyone who lives in our little makeshift community contributes, either with a job earning money, or doing work around the commune. I do the former, since manual labor isn't my strong suit. I'm more of an indoors-with-air-conditioning kind of worker myself.

Beth, the bank teller who works next to me, slams her drawer shut and loops her lanyard keychain around her wrist. "I'm taking a break," she mutters.

It's the first of the month, so today has been ridiculously

busy. My feet are sore from standing all day, and all I want to do is sneak in the back and eat my box of crackers, but we're short-handed and have a line all the way to the back, so I can't.

I nod at her distractedly as I continue counting money out to my customer. "Forty, sixty, eighty, one hundred."

The elderly woman in front of me takes her time re-counting everything. "There's only eighty dollars here," she accuses, shooting me a glare. "You're shorting me!"

I slide my hand over and separate the two bills that had stuck together. She glowers at me, as if I tricked her somehow. I shoot her a winning smile. "Is there anything else I can do for you today, Mrs. Lane?"

She grumbles something incoherent, swipes up her bills, and marches away. I still have a smirk on my face when I call for the next customer. "I can help the next person," I say, turning my face from the computer to greet them.

The smirk falls from my face when my nose detects his scent. A shifter, and not one from my pack. I immediately straighten up, my eyes scanning him from top to bottom. Nice clothes, blond hair, winning smile. Everything about him screams friendly guy next door, but I don't fall for it. I'm always wary of other shifters.

"How can I help you?" I ask, trying to force a smile back on my face. I've found that it's better to assess first as a friend, before being standoffish like a foe. But honestly, a lot of shifters do the exact opposite. We're very territorial and distrusting of outsiders by nature.

The shifter swaggers up to my teller window. "Hey. I need to take out some cash," he says, passing over a withdrawal slip and ID.

I completely ignore the fact that he's ridiculously hot. Okay, maybe not *completely*. But I have a great poker face about it. Honestly, I think it's his tan that really gets me going. I like it when a guy looks like he's been out in the sun instead of holed up indoors. There's something inherently sexy about it.

His blond hair and hazel eyes complement his skin tone nicely, but his face? It's lickable. And I don't go around wanting to lick just anybody. But him? I'd risk the germs for him.

I notice him taking me in as well, no doubt smelling that I'm a shifter, too. I ignore his perusal and take his withdrawal slip. I start typing away on my computer so I can get him taken care of as quickly as possible, because even though the guy is hot, he's still an outsider.

When I enter his account number and pull up his profile, my hand freezes on the keyboard because *whoa*. This guy is *loaded*.

I discreetly rub my eyes with my hand just to make sure the numbers aren't blurring together. Sometimes my mascara-covered lashes stick together and do that. But nope. There really are that many digits.

I quickly drop my hand and put on my *professional bank teller* face so that I can pretend like seven-digit numbers are totally normal. Boring, even. A millionaire? *Please.*

Same old, same old. If he's waiting for a reaction from me, he isn't going to get one. Professional. Bank. Teller.

I check his ID for his name. Penn Weiss. "Would you like that in hundreds, Mr. Weiss?" I ask him.

Did my voice just raise an octave?

God, I think my palms are sweating, too. One hot and tanned outsider with a ridiculously fat bank account, and I get all jittery, apparently. I don't know why, but rich people make me nervous. I didn't actually know this about myself until right this second, but hey, self-awareness is good. I may work at a bank, but I don't think I've ever seen someone have more than five digits at one time in this small town.

Mr. Seven Digits looks up at me from his phone. "Sure. You can throw in some twenties, too."

I nod quickly, attempting to look normal. "Okie dokie."

He snorts under his breath and shoots me a look. "Okie dokie?"

His hazel eyes twinkle with mockery. My own eyes narrow. Just like that, my nervousness is gone. "Are you making fun of me?"

The corner of his lip twitches. "I just haven't heard anyone say *okie dokie* since I was about seven."

"People say it all the time," I say vehemently. "Maybe you should get out more."

A grin splits across his face. *God, what kind of toothpaste is he using? His teeth are freaking sparkling.* "Tell you what, you let me know what time you get off, and you can make sure that I *get out more* when I pick you up tonight."

Now it's my turn to snort. "Yeah, no."

He tilts his head at me. "...Was that a yes or a no? You kinda said both."

"It's a no."

He clicks his tongue. "Eh, you said 'yeah' first, so I'm gonna go with that one."

I shake my head. "No, no you aren't. Because everyone knows that it's the *last* word you say that counts."

It's true. Ask anyone.

He leans forward and braces his forearms on the counter in front of me, and my eyes automatically dart down at his chest that's now on display. From what I can see, he's muscled and just as lickable down there. He also has an excellent collarbone. Not that I've checked out many collarbones. Or any, besides his. But still. His is top notch.

"Are you...looking down my shirt?" he asks, his voice filled with laughter.

I snap my eyes back up to his face. "What? No," I answer too quickly.

The asshole laughs at me, making my face heat up. I don't react well when people make fun of me. Call it a throw-back from a terrible childhood.

He flicks his hazel eyes to my nametag. "Okay, Aderyn

Locke. You're gonna have to buy me a drink for that down-the-shirt look you just stole."

I could try to deny it, but I'm no liar.

I shake my head. "Nice try."

He keeps the amused smile on his face as he looks around to see if anyone is near enough to overhear. Everyone else who works here is human, and I don't have the best sense of smell, but I'm fairly certain the rest of the customers in line are as well. When he's sure we won't be heard, he lowers his voice and says, "I can smell that you're a shifter."

"Huh," I say noncommittally, as I type more numbers into the computer. I'm not actually doing anything at this point. Fifty percent of this job is just pretending to do crap on the computer so that I can avoid awkward customer exchanges.

But the longer he stands in front of me, the more I smell him. I don't know what kind of shifter he is exactly, but Penn Weiss smells damn good. I'm not even one of those shifters that goes all scent-crazy, so that's saying something.

He lifts an arm to run his hand through his ashy blond hair. "Me and a couple of buddies just moved here. Used to be a part of the Moon Pack in Arizona," he says, importantly.

Ugh. Pack name dropping. I inwardly roll my eyes.

When I don't immediately gush, he pauses a bit and stuffs

his hands into his pockets, looking unsure. "You've heard of them, I assume?" he prods.

I pretend to be adequately impressed by smiling sweetly. "Of course. Every shifter in the western states has heard of them."

He grins cockily. The grin is nice. The cocky? Not so much.

His name-dropping does more than just let me know he's arrogant, though. It also clues me in to what type of shifter he is. The Moon Pack in Arizona is huge, made up of mostly wolves, bears, coyotes, and mountain lions.

"Yeah. We were some of the best enforcers they had. But we decided to branch out last year. Started traveling around on our own. We're wanting to relocate here with a smaller pack."

"How nice for you."

A line appears between his dark blond brows as he frowns at me. Oops. I guess I'm not doing so well at pretending to adequately fangirl. I'm sure he's used to shifter women going berserk over his famous former pack. Me? I'm just wary. I blink at him innocently before pulling out his cash and start counting it out to him. When I'm finished, he sticks the wad in his wallet.

"If you're finished, the line behind you is pretty long, and—"

"Actually," he cuts me off. "I need info about local packs. My buddies and I are looking to apply to join one. We'd be excellent assets," he says, and I swear, he flexes his muscles.

What a tool. A pretty tool, though. I'd like to handle his hammer.

"I'm sure you're very impressive," I say dryly.

His frown deepens. Yep. My pretend game is *definitely* weak. "Yeah…ummm, so anyway, what pack are you in?" he asks.

My expression immediately hardens and I abandon the fake smile altogether. I don't like it when anyone asks about my pack. Not because I'm ashamed, but because I'm protective as hell.

I know what happens when predator hotshots like this guy hear about Pack Aberrant. They laugh. They mock. They bully and throw challenges. It's why my pack had to move around so much, especially in the beginning, when numbers were low. We are somewhat notorious in the shifter world. Other shifters love to ridicule us.

But we've been in this territory now for ten years—as long as I've been a part of it. As long as the bigger asshole packs don't know where we are, they can't come in and challenge us for our land or kill our members.

Luckily, there's only one nearby—Pack Rockhead. Not so luckily, they're my old pack. I left as soon as I was of independent age, on my fifteenth birthday. To say that there's bad blood between us is putting it mildly. My blood relatives aren't my family. They haven't been since the first time I shifted. Pack Aberrant is more family to me than anyone that I share blood with.

"Why do you care what pack I'm in?" I ask.

He tilts his head to study me, probably wondering why I'm being so defensive. "Maybe I'm just curious."

"Well, I'm not here to satisfy your curiosity. I'm here to work."

His tawny eyebrows shoot up in surprise. "Whoa. Down girl," he says with amusement and a tugging grin. "You've got some bite. What are you? A wolf? Fox?"

Yep, I'm done with his questions. "Have a nice day, Mr. Weiss."

"Oh, come on," he says. "Look, I'm sorry we got off on the wrong foot. Let me start over. Hi," he says, holding out his hand.

I think about refusing to take it for a second, but then I see my manager watching me from his office. He likes to write people up if he finds that our interactions aren't friendly enough to customers. Grudgingly, I take his hand for a quick shake before dropping it right away, because as all shifters know, we have a thing for touching. It really riles us up. We're a touchy-feely lot, and sometimes, our animals can get attached.

"I'm Penn. Coyote shifter," he says, confirming my guess about him being a pred. "It's nice to meet you Aderyn Locke," he says like a damn gentleman. I narrow my eyes at him to show him that I don't appreciate it. He just smiles at me like he finds me adorable, which really raises my hackles. "I promise I'm not usually this bad at first impressions," he tells me.

"How do you know?" I challenge.

He gives me a look. "I'd know," he says assuredly.

"Maybe you give bad first impressions all the time, but you just don't know it because the other person always lets you down easy."

The corner of his mouth twitches. "Is that what you're doing, Aderyn? Letting me down easy?"

"If I was letting you down hard, you'd know," I say with excessive sweetness. "Have a good day." Then I turn to look at the next person waiting in line. "Next!"

He stays at my teller window and opens his mouth to argue, but when the next customer walks up behind him, he has no choice but to turn and leave with a grumble under his breath. I just bested a pred, and it feels pretty damn good. My lips tilt up in triumph...only to immediately fall back down when a gun is shoved into my face.

2

ADDIE

There's nothing like the view of a gun barrel in the middle of a workday. And to think, twenty minutes ago, I was yawning and thinking about taking a nap after work. Now that's out the window.

"Get your fucking hands up where I can see them!"

My wide eyes shoot across the bank to find that the shouted command is coming from a *second* gunman. Great.

I lift my nose in the air a bit to pick up their scent. Not shifters. Not any kind of Canes, in fact. They're both humans, and by the look of the one shouting at everyone to lay on the ground, they both have a superiority complex. You know the type—arms out, swinging like a gorilla, chin tilted up so that he can look down at everyone. He probably drives a lifted truck with tires big enough to haul around his huge sense of entitlement with him everywhere he goes. And when a dude has a big sense of entitlement, it usually means he has a very small...well, penis. There's no point in beating around the pube bush about it.

My eyes flick to Penn Weiss, Mr. Hotshot Coyote. He's currently on the ground near the door with the rest of the customers, but I can see his body is tense and ready for action.

As if he can feel my eyes on him, he suddenly glances over, his gaze locking with mine. When he sees that I have a gun currently pointed at my face, his lips curl back in a snarl. I try to give him a look to communicate with him not to do anything crazy, because that might make the gunmen panic and get the innocent humans shot.

"Hey, bitch," Gunman Number One says, waving the gun back and forth in front of my chest to regain my attention. Apparently, he doesn't like to be ignored.

"How can I help you?" I ask politely. Because I'm a professional bank teller even when I'm being robbed.

The gunmen are both wearing ski masks—how unoriginal —so I can't really see the face of the one in front of me except for his blue eyes. Make that *bloodshot* blue eyes, and his pupils are huge. This guy is higher than the waistband on mom jeans. Which means he'll be even more likely to react to things without thinking them through first.

"Open your fucking drawer," he orders, feeling pretty high and mighty behind his gun and mask.

I lean forward and try to get a sniff of him, but really, all I can pick up is some god-awful cologne. I think I wrinkle my nose on accident, so to cover up the reaction, I quickly grab my keys and sort through them for the right one. It takes me embarrassingly long, considering I've worked here for four months. But seriously, there are a shit ton of keys.

"Here it is," I chirp. I fit the key into the lock and...nope. Definitely not the right key. "Shoot," I say. Freezing, I look back up at the gunman. "Not *shoot* shoot, like the gun," I tell him quickly. "I meant shoot like shit. Bad word choice on my part," I mumble.

He just looks at me, unimpressed. "Bitch, open that drawer, or I *will* 'shoot shoot' you."

I smile nervously, trying to assuage the situation. "Right-o," I say. But then I do the dumbest thing ever and make a finger gun at him. I'm surprised at this point that he doesn't *actually* shoot me. Thankfully, the next key I slip in, successfully turns, allowing me to open the drawer.

With his other, non-gun wielding hand, the gunman tosses a plastic bag at my face, making it bounce off my cheek. "Empty your fucking drawer. Gimme all of it," he snaps.

My colleague, Beth, comes walking back out from the break room just as I start shoving the stacks of cash into the plastic bag. I try to signal her with my hand behind my back to go hide, but he notices her. "Hey, cunt, I see you! Get your ass over here and empty your drawer, too!"

Poor Beth hurries forward to her window, nearly tripping over her own feet when he continues to shout at her. Meanwhile, the other gunman is terrorizing all the bankers on the other side of the building, and I can see him hollering for my manager to come open the vault.

"There," I say, piling in the last of my cash. He snatches the bag from me and swings the gun to point it at Beth, who's shaking like a leaf as he continues to berate her.

When I see her start to cry, my blonde brows draw together in a frown and my eyes cut to the douche. "Dude, we're doing what you asked. Stop being such an asshole," I tell him.

In reply, the gunman rounds on me, and then lifts the gun to my head.

At. My. Head.

My lip curls up in rage, and just like that, I snap.

I move faster than he can blink. Using the ball of my palm, I smack his hand, making the gun point up. It startles him, so his trigger-happy finger pulls, and a shot rings out as the bullet cracks through the air and hits the ceiling. Screams sound out from terrified customers and employees, and drywall peppers down from above making the air dusty with damage.

But I'm already moving.

I reach across the counter, grab the guy by the back of his stupid mask, and slam the motherfucker's face into the counter so hard that I hear his nose break.

He screams and drops the gun onto the counter. Using the back of my hand, I fling it to the floor behind me. Then I leap onto the counter and jump down behind him to the other side. Blood is pouring from his nose and he's cradling it gingerly, but I quickly turn him around and knee him in the balls. He hits the ground with a screech.

"You fucking bitch!"

I only have about a second of triumph before *another* gun is pointed at my head by Gunman Number Two. I really don't like guns being pointed at my head.

"You're gonna pay for that, bitch!"

Gunman Number Two raises the butt of his gun to hit me, but before he can make contact with my head, he suddenly goes flying backwards and hits the floor hard. Penn has the man on his belly in a vicious chokehold before the gunman even knows what hit him. He tries to flail around, but Penn is way too strong. A lot of shifters can boast extra strength. I won't lie, seeing Penn's muscles flex as he overpowers the man is pretty hot. Unable to throw Penn off, the gunman finally succumbs, and he passes out cold. It all takes less than a minute.

Tossing the robber's prone body to the floor, Penn gets up and stalks over to the other gunman who's still cursing and bleeding at my feet. Penn rips off the guy's mask and shoves it into his mouth to muffle his voice. All it takes is one fierce scowl from him, and the gunman immediately stops making noise and lies down on the floor in surrender. It was a rather impressive scowl.

Penn snorts in disgust at him and then turns to me. His face looks furious, and he's doing this aggressive panting thing that for some reason really lights a fire in my loins.

"You okay?" he asks, looking me up and down.

"Yeah. Thanks for taking down Idiot Number Two."

"Any time. Although, it looked like you could've handled both," he says, his tone mixed with surprise and admiration.

I nod again. "I'm a badass."

He laughs, but when he sees that I'm serious, he tries to cough to cover it up.

"I wasn't joking," I insist. "I am a badass."

"Right. Of course," he quickly answers, but I can see that his hazel eyes are lit up with amusement.

"Do you want to fight?" I blurt.

His brows pull together. "What?"

"You don't think I could take you. I can see it in your eyes."

"Umm..." He rubs the back of his neck like he has no idea how to respond. He starts looking around the room, as if he's hoping another gunman will come along that he can take down as a distraction so he doesn't have to answer me.

"I *am* badass," I tell him again, because for some reason, I always like to have the last word.

The gunman at our feet sneezes, getting blood all over my shoes. I sigh. "These were my favorite pair," I tell him with a glower.

He mumbles something into the ski mask stuck in his mouth, as Penn looks down at my blood speckled feet. "Those don't seem like bank policy footwear," he teases.

I glance at my black Converse and shrug. "Customers can't see my feet when I'm behind my window."

"Let me buy you some new shoes," Penn says.

"I got these online."

He sighs and runs a thumb across his jaw with a chuckle. "Damn. You're a hard one to convince."

I'm not, really. I appreciate attractiveness as much as the next girl, but as a rule, I try to steer clear of predators like him. Luckily, I don't have to say anything else, because I'm saved by the flashing lights outside as the police come rushing in. They take one look at the overpowered robbers before quickly cuffing them and hauling them away, while the other cops start to organize everyone for questioning.

I sigh. There goes my early half-day. I'm gonna be stuck answering questions for a long time.

When the employees and customers are separated for questioning, I lose sight of Penn, which is for the best. He's excellent eye candy, but definitely not someone I want to mess with. Which is what I keep telling myself over and over again while my libido pouts in a corner.

All of the employees have to give written and verbal accounts for the police, which takes *forever.* By the time the cops' questions are satisfied, it's after five o'clock. All of the customers are long gone when the employees finally get permission to leave. Before I can make my escape, my manager pulls me aside.

He's an okay guy. Balding and nasally, Tom sports a hefty belly over his dress pants. "Ms. Locke, if you could come into my office please?"

Beth shoots me a sympathetic look and waves goodbye to me as I inwardly groan. "Sure thing, boss."

I follow Tom into his office and he shuts the door behind us. When he sits down behind his desk, he sighs. "Aderyn, I have to let you go."

I blanche at him, completely taken aback. "What? Why?"

He gives me a look. "You know protocol. You broke just about every single rule we have when it comes to dealing with a robbery. Your actions put yourself and everyone in the bank in danger."

I scoff and lean back in the chair. "I wasn't going to let them shoot anyone, including me. Besides, I handed him the money like I was supposed to."

"You were belligerent. You talked back and you provoked him."

"He was making Beth cry!"

"And *then* you attacked him," he reminds me, unimpressed.

"Well, yeah. He pointed a gun at my face. How was I supposed to respond?"

Tom shakes his head in frustration. "I'll tell you how you

shouldn't have responded! You shouldn't have attacked him and made the gun go off! You're supposed to put your hands up and surrender like a normal human being."

I am neither normal nor a human. But of course, I don't say that. "I'm sorry, alright?"

He shakes his head. "This is out of my hands, Aderyn. Your actions are all over surveillance. The bank won't keep you on. You're too much of a liability."

My stomach turns in knots. Dammit, I really need this job. My alpha is gonna be so pissed.

I grit my teeth. "Fine. Thank you for the opportunity," I say levelly.

Getting up, I toss him my keys before opening the door to leave.

"You'll get your final check in the mail," he says to my back.

"Thanks," I mumble under my breath.

Today is just not my fucking day.

3

ADDIE

I stare up at the cloudy night sky as I float on my back. The water laps around me gently and I sigh in relaxation. After the bank robbery and getting fired, driving down to the lake was exactly what I needed. No matter what's going on in my life, the water always calms me.

I close my eyes and submerge myself completely for a few moments. Blackmuck Lake might have a terrible name, but the fresh water and the quiet location are perfect for decompressing. During the day, there's a nice view of the mountains and the trees to give the perfect amount of privacy, and usually, this place is only known to the locals.

As soon as I break the water again and take in a deep breath, I'm startled out of my thoughts.

"Aren't you cold in there?"

I turn my head at the sudden voice and see a dark-skinned guy standing at the edge of the lake. I can't see very well at night, not compared to most shifters, but I can tell from his silhouette that he's packing some serious muscles.

"Nope," I answer.

He bends down and flicks his hand in the water and makes a face as he wipes it off on his pant leg. "It's definitely not warm," he says, as if the temperature personally offends him.

I snort. "It's a lake, not a jacuzzi."

"I have no idea how your teeth aren't chattering," he says, and damn, his voice is all low and sexy.

"I guess only the strongest can handle it."

He chuckles, and the sound sends a thrill through me. I start wading closer to him so that I can get a better look. When I'm within a few feet of him, my nose tells me what I'd already figured. He's a shifter. He points his own nose up in the air too, obviously picking up that I'm a shifter as well. When he catches the scent, for a moment, I see his eyes flash, even in the dark, and I wonder what kind of animal lives inside of him.

He crouches down on the balls of his feet and lets his hand swipe through the water again, like he's trying to see how long it'll take for the temperature to not bother him. Hopefully he's a good dude. If it turns out he has nefarious plans for me, then I'll have to go all badass on him and pull him into the lake. Clearly, his type of shifter doesn't appreciate large bodies of water, so I could probably hop out and make a run for the campsite on the other side of the water.

I swim nearer, and he rests his hands on his bent knees from the spot where he's positioned. Under the moonlight, I can see his eyes tracking my movement and studying my features. "Most shifters don't like the water," he says as my feet hit the rocky sand and I start moving forward.

That's not exactly true. What he means is, most warm-blooded predator shifters don't like water. But I'm sure that's the only kind of shifters he thinks about. I shrug a shoulder and skim the water against my palms. "I'm not like most shifters."

A slow smile spreads across his face and his perfect teeth practically glow in the dark. "I'm Herrick. You must be in Pack Rockhead," he wrongly assumes. I don't correct him.

If he thinks I'm from that pack, then he must not be a part of it. Which means he's another newcomer, just like Mr. Millionaire Hotshot Coyote, Penn Weiss. My guess is that Herrick is one of the "buddies" that Penn mentioned.

"It's gonna rain soon," Herrick says, looking up just as the clouds start to thunder above us.

"You don't like lakes *or* rain?" I tease. "Do you hate showers, too? Are you like those miserable cats when they accidentally fall into the bathtub?"

He crosses his arms and flashes a grin. "I have no problem with a wet pussy."

I snort and swallow a laugh. "After all your anti-wetness talk, I don't have a lot of confidence in you," I say wryly.

As I continue wading to shore, I watch as he scoops water

up in his palm and then tips his hand over to let it leak back out. Some of the water escapes his palm and slowly drips down his forearm, dripping off his bare elbow. I have no idea why, but watching it trickle down his skin is oddly erotic.

Most shifters are well-defined naturally, but Herrick is ripped with muscles, and I ogle his bicep a bit longer than I probably should. When he dips his hand in the water to do it again, my eyes follow every slow movement.

"See?" he says, drawing my gaze back to his face. "My hands are good at getting things wet."

I laugh and groan at the same time, but I can't deny that his words send a little excited thrill through me. "Hmm," I say noncommittally.

When thunder erupts over head, we both look up at the sky, watching the impending storm gather. I float around for a little while longer, mostly trying to wait Herrick out. I'm not ashamed of my body or anything, but my animal is wary of strangers and she doesn't want me to leave the water. When the thunder starts to sound more serious, though, I decide it's time to go, despite my animal's proclivity for wanting to stay.

Herrick watches me as I walk the rest of the way out of the water, and his attention kicks my heart rate up a notch and heats me up in the best of ways. I spot the towel that I'd left out several feet away in a pile along with my clothes. I feel his gaze burning into my back (AKA bikini-clad ass) as I walk over and pick it up. I start drying my body off with the towel, before using it to wring out my blonde hair.

All the while, he continues to watch from his spot where he's still kneeling, but instead of it feeling weird, there's this undeniable magnetism between us that makes his attention welcome.

I don't know where I get the confidence, but I find myself wanting to give him a little show, so I slowly bend over to retrieve my things before tugging an oversized shirt on and turning back around to face him. I'm pretty sure I hear a groan of appreciation grumbling from his chest.

I catch him taking in my bare legs and the white t-shirt where it sticks to my green bikini top, and my lips twitch at his expression. "See you around, Herrick," I say before turning to leave.

As soon as I start to walk away, I hear him take a few jogging steps to catch up with me. "Hey, wait up. Leaving so soon?"

"Oh, you know, things to not do, people to not see."

Herrick chuckles again and walks backwards in front of me. "Can I get your number?"

"I'm mated," I answer automatically. Not because it's true, but because this guy...let's just say I'm not his type. And that's not me being self-deprecating. It's just true. He's a predator and a total hottie. I'm a misfit. We might both be shifters, but we practically come from two different worlds.

At hearing that I'm mated, his steps falter for a second

before he turns to walk beside me. He leans in close and takes a big whiff of my scent. "No, you're not," he counters.

"Oh, did I say mated? I meant not interested."

He laughs, and I can't stop the smile that spreads over my face from the sound of it. "Alright, alright," he concedes. "I see you like to play hard to get."

I let my gaze fall to the front of his pants. "And it looks like you like to play *get hard.*"

This time when he laughs, he tips his head back and lets loose loud enough to echo with the thunder. The sound follows me as he hangs back. "I'm sure I'll see you again, Lake Lady," he calls.

"I'll be sure to bring a spray bottle to keep you away," I say over my shoulder.

His laugh tapers off with the thunder, and by the time I get to my beat-up Nissan, the skies have opened up and the rain is pouring down hard. Of course, the rain wouldn't be an issue if I didn't have a busted window that doesn't roll up all the way. I spend the entire drive getting pelted by rain drops, soaking the interior of my car. Not that it's really hurting much. The car is older than me, and has so many miles on it that the odometer has stopped working.

By the time I get to the Aberrant compound, the fabric of the seats are squishing and there's a good inch of water on the floorboards. I was already wet from the lake, but the rain doused me so much that my hair is plastered to my face and I'm seriously regretting this white t-shirt.

I idle the car as I reach the grounds' gates. The enforcers take shifts to stand watch at the guard tower, which, luckily for them, is completely enclosed. I shield my eyes with a hand so that I can look up at the tower without raindrops pelting my eyeballs.

A flashlight shines in my eyes before I hear Stinger over the intercom. "You're lookin' a little wet, Addie," he jokes. "I bet you're wishing you would've listened to Alpha when he told you to tape that window up, huh?"

I put my hand out the window and toss up my middle finger. He just laughs, and then he buzzes the gate door open and I drive through with a wave.

Our compound is a pretty good size now, with multiple structures all over the property. To the right are all the cabins for the mated shifters and families, and straight ahead is the alpha's house and some of the shared spaces, like the gym and the hall we use when we all gather to eat together or celebrate.

I turn onto the dirt road on the left, where the singles' housing is. All the single shifters live in one of the large, boxy buildings that we lovingly call the warehouses. They aren't very traditionally pretty from the outside, but they do have a cool, urban feel to them that I dig. Especially given that one of our shifters has a propensity for decorating them with graffiti. It's usually some pretty funny shit, but none of us have guessed who's actually the one doing the tagging.

I pull off the road to head to the third warehouse and fit my car under the wooden carport alongside the others. Shielding my car from the rain is kind of a moot point by now, but oh, well.

I grab my purse and my bag with all of my work clothes, and run across the yard to head for the front door. The interior of the warehouse that I call home has polished concrete floors and exposed industrial piping on the ceiling. There are two stories and a metal catwalk that spans the entire side, bookended by staircases.

The ground floor is wide-open, so I can see the gaming area in one corner, the kitchen and dining area in the other, and the lounge space as soon as I walk inside. The bedrooms and bathrooms are upstairs. The rooms are small, and we only have four bathrooms between us, but it's not so bad.

"Aderyn Locke, you're late!"

I slip my wet, muddy flip flops off and look up to where Zoey is yelling at me from the catwalk. Her hands are braced on the railing, and she's arching a brow at me.

"I know," I say, making my way across, heading to the stairs. I see a couple of the guys playing video games on the couch, and I toss them a wave as I start ascending. "I went to the lake after work," I explain.

Zoey takes in my soaked t-shirt and cocks her head. "Uh oh. What happened?"

"How do you know something happened?"

"Puhlease." She rolls her eyes as she leans on the railing.

"You always go wade around when something is bothering you."

She has me there. "Robbery at the bank," I admit.

Her mouth drops open, making a pretty comical "O," and she straightens up. "Oh, shit. You okay?"

"Yeah, except I got fired."

"Oh no! Why?"

I walk past her and she follows me into our room that we share. "I may have…sort of attacked the robber."

She nods like this is perfectly acceptable. "Good for you, girl."

Once inside our room, I shut the door and start peeling off my dripping shirt and bathing suit. It doesn't even phase us to be naked around each other since we shift so much in here. "Not to the humans. They fired me for it."

"Oh. Shit."

"Yeah."

Zoey tucks her sleek black hair behind her ear. She's a rattlesnake shifter, except she was born without a rattle. All of the members in her pack over in New Mexico viewed her as defective, and none of the males would give her the time of day. She came here about nine months ago, and she's been dating it up ever since. Her current boyfriend lives in the warehouse next door.

"Well, screw them. Hugo will understand, and you'll get another job."

The prospect of having to apply for new jobs makes me groan. "I hate interviewing. I always get nervous and my palms get all sweaty."

"Wear pants. Then all you have to do is wipe them down before you shake hands. Problem solved."

"Thanks for bestowing your wisdom," I say dryly.

Zoey's eyes suddenly light up. "Oh my gosh! You know what I just realized?" she asks excitedly.

I riffle through the clothes in my drawer and pull on some shorts and a tee before I hang my wet stuff up in the shower. "What?" I ask her, walking back into the bedroom.

"No more strict dress code! That means you can dye your hair like you've always wanted to," she says excitedly.

She's a hair stylist down at Cupid Cuts, so she comes home with a new hairdo about once a month. We've been talking about dyeing my hair fun colors since she first got here, but I've always had strict office jobs that disallowed it. My blonde hair is long, light, and naturally wavy. And aside from the occasional trim at the ends, completely untouched. I've been wanting a change, and now, it seems like I'll finally get the chance.

A smile pulls at the side of my lips as I look over at her. "Are you thinking what I'm thinking?"

She clasps her hands together hopefully. "Pastel unicorn hair?"

I nod. "Pastel motherfuckin' unicorn hair."

4

ADDIE

I manage to avoid telling Hugo that I got fired for five whole days.

I fully enjoy my reprieve from adulting for that entire span of time. Without a job, I don't have to get up early, which means I don't have to go to sleep early, which means I pretty much just end up binge watching Netflix on my laptop all night and stay in my pajamas all day. Day pajamas are awesome. No shoes, no bra, no pants, no probs. I'm living the dream.

My friend slash roommate doesn't really agree, I guess, because on her way out to work this morning, Zoey took one look at the chip stains on my pillow and my sloppy appearance, and lovingly called me a hobo who needed to shower before she got home or she'd hose me down. I fell back asleep instead.

My lazy ass is snoring into my pillow when a loud banging rings out, jarring me awake. I shove the pillow

over my head to drown it out, but the banging just continues. One thing about living in a warehouse, it's not sound-
proof. Everything echoes.

I throw off the pillow and groan. Standing up, I wipe the
drool from my chin and head for the door. I trip out of
my room, slip down several steps of the stairs, and then
drag myself to the front door, throwing it open with a
scowl, ready to tell off whoever it is that woke me up. I
hadn't gone to sleep until four AM this morning, after a
binge-fest of *Schitt's Creek*, so I was planning on a solid
thirteen-hour nap today.

But when I see that it's Hugo, the alpha of my pack,
standing there with his arms crossed, I quickly replace my
scowl with a smile. "Oh. Hugo!"

He rolls his eyes. "Don't even try that smiley shit on me,"
Hugo says. "When were you gonna tell me you were held
at gunpoint and robbed?"

Hugo is like a father to me, so I feel instantly chagrined. I
look down and shuffle my feet. "I got fired. I didn't want
you to be disappointed in me," I mumble.

He snorts, and I peek up to look at him through my—
admittedly crusty—lashes. Hugo is a big son of a bitch,
and he has scars littering his exposed arms. He always
wears a leather vest and blue jeans like he's in some kind
of biker gang, even though the closest he's gotten to a bike
is walking by the stationary one in the gym. He's tough,
rough around the edges, and he doesn't take any shit, but
he's also fair and loyal as hell.

Hugo sets his heavy hand on my shoulder. "Now look

here you little shit," he says sternly. "I don't give a fuck about the job, but if someone points a gun at a member of my pack, I need to know."

I fake-punch him on the arm. "Aww, you're getting all alpha-fatherly protective!" I tease.

He ignores my playful tone and studies me. "You okay, Addie?"

I drop the playfulness and nod seriously. "Yeah, peachy keen. No worries. I took the asshole down."

He smirks and scratches the scruffy brown beard at his chin. "I heard. Guess those self-defense lessons you whined about really took."

My lips curve. "Guess they did."

I watch his eyes dart over my hair. "What the hell did you let Zoey do to you?"

I thread my pastel blue, pink, purple, green, and blonde hair through my fingers. "Isn't it pretty?" I singsong. Aside from giving me pastel unicorn hair to mix with my blonde locks, she also trimmed it, so now I have a cooler, shorter cut.

"It looks like you got into a fight with a cotton candy machine. And lost."

I nod. "Like I said. Pretty."

He snorts, but then his face turns serious. "Listen, we've been having some trouble with the Rockheads. They've been giving a few of our members some trouble in town. I want you to keep your eyes open and I'm telling everyone not to go out alone."

My blonde brows shoot up in surprise. "That doesn't sound good. What kind of trouble?"

"Nothin' you need to worry about, kid. Just keep your head down same as everyone else, and don't leave pack territory without at least one other member."

He says not to worry, but I'm not so sure. I grew up in Pack Rockhead, after all. I know what they're like. I clear my throat awkwardly. "What kinds of things are they doing?"

"You know their M.O. The fuckers like to toss around their pred status like it grows their dicks an inch every time," Hugo said, making me snort in laughter. "A trio of them cornered Stinger the other night at the gas station. Things nearly got physical, but the human police happened to show up, so Rockhead bailed. Then a couple more of the fuckwads were heckling Trudy when she was at the community pool. Luckily, some of the human regulars stepped in. They told the Rockheads to back off."

"Shit. They haven't bothered to mess with us this much before. Not even when I left," I say, more to myself than to him. "I wonder what's changed all of a sudden."

Hugo shrugs his bulky shoulders. "Don't know. But I intend to find out. Until I do, our pack needs to be smart and stay safe."

I nod distractedly, feeling unease in the pit of my stomach. I prefer to pretend that Rockhead doesn't exist at all. I've become pretty good at it, actually. My family wants nothing to do with me, and I want nothing to do with them. But my old pack is terrorizing my current pack, and it brings up a lot of bad memories.

Hugo eyes me quietly, no doubt reading my every expression. As an alpha, he's adept at reading his pack member's emotions. "You sure you're okay, kid?"

I force myself to smile. "Totally fine. I had the bank robbery under control."

"I had no doubt in my mind," he replies proudly.

"Oh, I should probably mention that I saw a couple of outsiders. One at the bank and one at the lake afterward. Pred shifters who left the Moon Pack in Arizona."

He grunts in disapproval. Like me, he's not fond of predators who come sniffing around our territory.

"I wonder if Rockhead is recruiting them," he muses.

I shake my head. "I don't think so. It sounded like they just ventured over here on their own. But I'm sure they'll end up with Rockhead."

He snorts. "Asshole preds always do," he says. His phone vibrates in his pocket, and he digs it out, swiping his finger across the screen and then frowns at it with a sigh. "Gunter got stuck on the electric pole."

"Again?" I ask, exasperated.

"Yup." He shoves his phone back into his pocket and looks back up at me. "I gotta go take care of this. You sure you're okay? And you'll be safe?"

"Sure thing, jelly bean."

"Speaking of jelly beans, you have candy stuck to you," he points out and sure enough, there's a lollipop, stick and all, hanging at the bottom of my wrinkled shirt. "And it's noon, Addie. This ain't a respectable time to still be sleeping. Either get a job, or I'll put you to work around here. Then you can be the one to rescue Gunter when his squirrel climbs up that damn pole and then gets too scared to come down."

I wrinkle my nose. "No need to make threats, Alpha. I'll get a job."

He snorts and starts walking toward his Jeep. "You do that, kid. And if anyone else gives you trouble, I need to hear about it first."

"Yes sir, Alpha Hugo, sir."

I head back inside to shower. Guess it's time to start hunting for a job.

ADDIE

"Come again?"

I look over at Zoey from where she's perched on her bed. She has her black hair in an elaborate dutch braid that's wrapped around her head like a crown. "Are you really gonna make me say it again?" I groan.

She smiles, showing off her small and slightly sharp fangs. Usually, they look cute, but right now, it makes her look downright impish. "Yep."

I sigh. "I said, I got hired at *Doggie Style Pet Shop.*"

She bursts out laughing, snorts and all. She laughs so hard that her fangs start spraying out venom. We watch as it arcs onto the floor, sending a spurt of toxins in the carpet. I once made her a bet that she couldn't spray it more than three feet. I lost.

"It's not that funny," I say dryly, but she just continues her cackling. "Keep it up, and I'll put your snakey ass in a cage and sell you on my first day. For a discount."

She just laughs harder, so I chuck a pillow at her head. She instantly retaliates by throwing her massive body pillow at me, making me knock into the wall behind me and smack the back of my head.

Of course, I throw it right back, quicker than she can anticipate, hitting her square in the face. I can't help but smile with victory as I grab another pillow, ready for her to retaliate.

"Huh. I thought all of that talk about pillow fights between girls was exaggerated for the benefit of males everywhere. I for one am glad to see that it's real."

I peer over the pillow I had held up like a shield and see Zoey's boyfriend, Matt, standing in our doorway. Zoey, still laughing, jumps up and goes over to give him a kiss, but not before decking me with another pillow.

"Hey!" I try to throw it back at her, but she darts behind Matt and I end up hitting him in the head instead. "Whoops. Sorry, Matt."

Luckily, he doesn't mind being used as a pillow shield or catching the brunt of my attack, even though it knocks his glasses off.

Matt is the best kind of nerd. He's lanky and wears glasses, and he has fluffy black hair and the whole hipster look on lockdown. He's always in some kind of graphic t-shirt and playing video games on his computer. But he's kind and he's good to Zoey, which is what I mostly care about. He seems to be a good fit for her, even though she's adamant that they're just having fun for now.

I've only ever seen him do it one time, but when he shifts, he's a three-legged otter. Some kind of accident forced an amputation, and now he hates shifting. His old pack was pretty awful to him from what I've heard. But not shifting is dangerous for us. If we keep our animals locked inside of us for too long, they can grow feral. Hugo is always talking about the importance of showing your animal respect, and letting them take the reins sometimes.

For now, Matt only shifts in private, but it's something Hugo is working on with him. Our alpha is big on embracing our differences, and I know Zoey is support- ive, so I have no doubt that he'll get past his holdups. Besides, I think otters are cool as shit.

"Sorry to interrupt the war," Matt says, catching the pillow and tossing it back on my bed. He fixes his glasses while Zoey peeks out from behind him, smirking like a brat. "Some of us are going to the club. You guys wanna go?" he asks.

Zoey and I are already nodding our heads and making a beeline toward our closet before he can even finish his sentence. Fifteen minutes later, about twenty of us singles are piling into our cars and heading off of pack territory to drive into town.

The night sky is crisp and clear, and I'm happily riding in Zoey's car, listening to her talk about a client at work that she had to talk out of getting a bowl cut. It's eight o'clock on the dot when we pull up into the parking lot for our favorite hang out, and our group heads into *Club Joystick.* Yep. We go to a gamer club. Us misfits are cool like that.

The inside is a huge space filled with computers, flat screens, skee ball, pool, air hockey, and dozens upon dozens of old school arcade games. I can just breathe in the awesome '90s nostalgia in the air. The best part about *Club Joystick* is every Thursday night from seven to midnight, the whole place is adult-only. Games, beer, inappropriate music, and a shit ton of pizza awaits us. It's perfect.

Zoey and Matt go off for a knock-down, drag-out air hockey competition, while I go play *PacMan* with another one of our friends, Aspen. She's a cool chick, and she stays on pack land and runs the homeschool program for the younger shifter kids. Since we shift sporadically as children, we can't go to human school until we get our shifting under control and learn to hide our animals.

Aspen lives in one of the other singles' warehouses, and is probably the most adorable person I've ever seen. Not that I would tell her that to her face. I once saw Stinger call her cute, and Mr. Enforcer walked away with a limp. Aspen is about five foot even, has brown hair, dimples in her cheeks, and her two front teeth are big, but somehow it makes her smile even more perfect. Like I said, adorable, and her sweet voice doesn't help things. But I've faced her in the training ring when Hugo runs defensive fighting drills, and she is a force to be reckoned with.

"How do those little ghosts never get you?" I ask with exasperation.

"PacMan is my jam," she replies as she moves the joystick with more finesse than I thought possible. She handles the joystick so well in fact, that I notice a few of the guys shooting her appreciative glances. Men.

We take turns at the game, but after the second round, there's no coming back for me. Her score is ridiculously high, whereas mine is...not. "You bitch," I tell her.

Aspen laughs and just tosses more quarters into the machine, never taking her eyes off it. "Sorry, Addie. Better luck next time."

She's even adorable when she wins. Instead of rubbing it in my face like I've been known to do, she preens gracefully. I hate losing. I need to rectify the feeling immediately, so I go to the one machine that never lets me down. I shoot Zoey a thumbs up when I see her score is a point higher than Matt's at the air hockey table, and continue making my way through the arcade.

When I spot my favorite game, my lips curl upward. "Come to mama."

Within minutes, I'm annihilating anyone who tries to beat my score. I'm in the zone and passing out some mad trash talk when I feel a tap on my shoulder. I look over to see an attractive guy smirking down at me. "You're pretty good at that," he says, tipping his head at the padded mallet in my hand.

"Yeah. I'm pretty good at whacking the mole," I say. Then I cringe because, yeah. That sounded dirtier than I intended.

The guy laughs. "I'm Mario Perez," he offers, holding out his hand.

I shake his hand, feeling his warm, firm grip. I know immediately that he's a human, but unlike a lot of shifters, I'm not against having fun outside of my species. "I'm Addie."

His dark brown eyes slide over me, but not in a creepy way. "Don't you work at the bank?" he asks. He doesn't seem familiar, but I would see hundreds of customers every week, so he might've slipped through the cracks of my memory.

"Yeah. Not anymore, though," I answer, dropping the mallet and trying to contain the fist pump I want to throw in the air at my new high score. I have to play this cool.

"Why not?" he asks.

I look longingly at my high score, the beeping like music to my ears, and force myself to focus on him. Would it be weird to pull out my phone and take a picture to save this momentous occasion? He'd probably think it was weird. Still, my fingers are itching to grab my phone and do it anyway. "Oh. It's a long story," I mumble distractedly.

He looks between me and the scoreboard I'm staring at. "Yeah?" he prompts.

I feel the seconds tick down like my own personal count-down. Every second makes me twitch until I can't stand it anymore. To hell with it. I dig into my pocket, yank out my phone, and open my camera. Selfie-style, I snap a pic with my beaming face as I throw up a finger to point at the obnoxiously large red numbers showing my high score. Mario just looks at me awkwardly as I snap the picture.

No regrets.

A second after I get the pic, the scoreboard goes blank and the exciting beeps cut off. Thank goodness I got it in time. That was a close one. I can't wait to show Zoey and Aspen later. Why is it that when a cute guy finally talks to me, it's right in the midst of my arcade glory that he clearly doesn't understand?

"I heard they just had a robbery."

His words bring me back to our conversation that I'm admittedly sucking at. Mingling and small talk is not my thing. But really, it's part of the misfit M.O. "Oh, yeah. I was there when it happened."

He eyes me curiously for a moment. "That had to have been scary."

I shrug. "Yeah. I don't recommend participating in one."

He smiles slightly, showing off nice teeth. He really is nice to look at for a human. He has mocha skin and jet black hair, and a solid four inches on me. "Sorry that you had to go through that."

"Eh, stuff happens. It could've been worse."

"I guess that's true," he agreed.

Awkward silence descends between us, and I start to tug at the hem of my shirt while looking around, desperately trying to find a way to escape. I'm terrible with guys. You know those genes that some girls have, making them able to talk to anyone and turn heads? Yeah, I don't have that. Those are some designer-type genes. My genes have holes in them. Bottom-shelf type of stuff.

I try to catch Aspen's eye, but she's playing *Centipede* with one of the guys, and I don't see Zoey anywhere. I'm debating about whether or not it would make this weirder if I excused myself to the bathroom, but Mario clears his throat before I can decide. "I've never been here before," he admits.

I chuckle and look at him again. I give his slacks and button up shirt a once-over. "I can see that."

He looks down at his own outfit and runs his hands down his shirt with a bemused smile. "Is it that bad?"

I tilt my head to the side. "You look like you're going to start pulling people aside and offer to do their taxes."

He chuckles, and the sound warms me up enough to make some of the awkwardness fall away.

"So, Addie, how about you show me how to play this game and I'll buy you a beer?"

I smile. Now this, I can do. "By the time I'm done with you, Mario, you'll be so good at whacking the mole, all the other whackers will be jealous."

He chokes out a laugh. "I've never had a girl who wanted me to whack *more*. How can I resist an offer like that?"

We spend the next three hours playing. The first hour is spent with me showing him all the secrets of the mallet and sipping on cheap beer while we eat pizza between turns. When it's clear he's never going to excel at mole whacking, we move onto *Frogger* and then *Street Fighter*. I win at everything. It's an excellent ego boost after getting trampled by Aspen.

The place is winding down, and some of my packmates have already left.

"Can I take you out? We could move onto a different kind of club," he offers as we make our way to the door. My stomach is whining at me from eating and drinking so much. I probably shouldn't have had that fifth slice of pizza. "I'm kind of beat," I admit, giving him a sideways smile. "My ride is about to leave, so I'd better go, but maybe another time?"

He looks disappointed, but quickly recovers as we exchange phone numbers. "How about tomorrow? We could meet at *Dare*."

That trendy restaurant bar isn't really my scene, but he's cute, nice, and…I haven't gotten laid in months. The last time was just a one-night stand with a tourist and the guy was less than impressive. Plus, I can feel my heatwave approaching. It happens a couple of times a year for shifters, and it's *intense*. Like embarrassing mewling, moaning, and I've even been known to beg.

At least if I spend it with Mario, I won't just be falling into some stranger's bed to sate my animalistic needs. Admittedly, humans aren't the best companions to help ride out the wave, but it's better than being alone.

"Okay, sure," I relent. Really, my vagina is calling the shots at this point.

He beams. "You want me to pick you up?"

"That's okay, I'll meet you there. Maybe we can make it a double date? I'll bring a couple friends."

His smile falters, but he's polite enough to play it off. "Sure. I'll meet you there at eight?"

"Sounds good."

"Hey, there you are!" Zoey says, sidling up to me with a triumphant grin on her face. I also notice that her pony-tail is slightly skewed, with hair sticking out at the top of her head. "I kicked Matt's ass so hard tonight. You couldn't get me away from that machine," she brags proudly.

"I saw you guys disappear for an hour to the bathroom," I say dryly.

She just shrugs. "What can I say? Winning makes me hungry. And not for pizza," she says, winking.

I roll my eyes.

"Who's your friend?" she asks, looking over Mario curiously.

"I'm the guy that Addie tried teaching video games to all night," he says smoothly, holding out his hand for her to shake.

"You must not be very good then," she replies.

"Hey!" I say indignantly, pinching her on the arm. She swats me away.

"Ready to go?" she asks.

"Yeah. You and Matt up for a double date tomorrow at *Dare?*"

Her eyes light up. "Ohh they have the best canapes. Can't wait!"

I turn back to Mario. "See you tomorrow?"

"Yep. Goodnight, ladies," he offers.

I give Mario a wave and then Zoey and I make our way through the arcade toward the doors. She elbows me as soon as we're outside. "The human, huh?"

I shrug. "He's nice enough."

She smirks at me and pulls out her ponytail, running her fingers through her messed up hair. "Hot enough, too?"

"Shut up. My heatwave isn't due for another couple of weeks or so."

She sighs languorously with a dreamy look on her face as we approach her car. "I love being in heat. It's so…"

"Licentious? Reckless? Slutty?" I supply.

She frowns. "I was gonna say special."

I snort as I get in the car and she starts it up. "You would, you hornball. You snakes are the reason for the fall of all mankind."

She lifts a shoulder as she buckles her seatbelt. "What can

I say? We like to tempt." She licks her lip suggestively and wags her eyebrows. She reaches over and puts her hand against my forehead and then makes a weird hissing/clicking sound as she drops her hand. "Yeesh. You're wrong, girl. You're going into heat sooner than a couple of weeks." Zoey is sensitive to temperature, but I'm not convinced. I don't feel *that* far gone yet.

"We'll see," I say as she pulls out of the parking lot to head back to pack land.

She gives me a superior look. "Yep. We *will* see. And then I'll say I told you so and you'll have to wear your, *Addie was wrong* sweatshirt for an entire weekend."

I hated that damn sweatshirt.

I roll my eyes. *"If* you're right, then I guess it's a good thing I met Mario Perez."

Zoey claps her hands excitedly. "Yay for sexy times!"

My vagina claps with her. She couldn't agree more.

6
ADDIE

I'm cheering along with everyone else in the audience as the live band finishes their song. Despite the fact that I usually avoid *Dare* since it's such a popular place, the music isn't bad and Zoey was right—the canapes are delicious. I didn't even know what a canape was until she ordered them as appetizers, but now I'm hooked.

Zoey and Matt are sitting with me and Mario at a tall circular table. I'm glad I did the whole double date thing. You know, just in case Mario turned out to be a psycho. Or an ass. Or boring. Any of those would've been a real downer. Luckily, he's been pretty fun all night, and I've only embarrassed myself once when I accidentally snorted at a joke Matt made about hard drives. Nobody else got it. Such a waste.

The place is packed like I knew it would be, and we're sitting at a table near the bar where the crowd is a little rowdier, and waitresses keep rushing past us back and forth to serve drinks and food to the rest of the bar. The atmosphere is all navy blue and black, with a waterfall for a wall behind the bar, and exposed steel pipes on the ceiling. The acoustics bounce off the spacious walls despite how many bodies are inside, and there's a good mix of drinking, eating, and dancing.

I tried to leave the house in jeans and a t-shirt, but Zoey took one look at me and threatened to bite me unless I went back into our closet and let her dress me. And trust me, no one wants to be bitten by Zoey, in snake form or otherwise. Her small, sharp teeth are vicious. The last time she threatened to bite me was over the last cookie in our stash. I ate it. She bit me. She even let a little venom seep into it. She was *that* serious about the damn cookie.

So yeah, I relented and I changed my outfit. Now, I'm in a black minidress and cobalt heels that are decidedly *not* comfortable like the sneakers with my previous outfit. Plus, my dress keeps riding up, so I'm worried that at some point in the evening, my vagina is going to make an accidental debut. The shoes are killing my feet too, but they do make my legs and butt look good, so there's that at least.

It didn't escape my notice that Zoey left the house in a fake skirt. You know the kind—the shorts that have lace wrapped around them to make it look like a skirt. She totally cheated, and there will be hell to pay about it later. If she makes me suffer like this, the least she could do was suffer with me. But no, she's sitting there with her legs uncrossed, looking comfy as hell with her heeled boots as she swings her legs without a care for her vagina making a surprise appearance. Traitor.

I eye Mario's tan slacks and white button up shirt. It's a nice contrast to his darker skin, and he looks nice in it, even if it's not the normal look I go for. I usually gravitate to the dudes in jeans and obscure t-shirts, maybe messy hair and some scruff, but it's not like I have guys lining up at my door, so who am I to be choosey?

"So, Addie, you mentioned you were at the bank robbery the other day," Mario says, leaning over slightly.

"That's right."

The band starts playing again, making it harder to hear, and Zoey waves over the waitress to order some dessert. "Did you recognize the guys?" Mario asks, raising his voice a bit.

I shake my head and run a finger over the rim of my empty glass. "Nope, never seen them before. I would've remembered that aura of stupidity that hovered around them."

Mario laughed lightly. "Is it true you actually hit one of them?" he asks, leaning in even closer.

For some reason, his human scent washes over me and makes my nose burn. I have to discreetly itch it to get the feeling to go away. "Hit is a strong word," I say, trying really hard not to sneeze.

"So you didn't hit him?"

"Oh, no, I hit him. I was just pointing out that the word choice was strong."

He doesn't seem to know what to do about my dry sense of humor, so the bad joke just shrivels up and flakes away.

"Right," he finally says, and I'm grateful as hell when the waitress comes back and brings up a round of chocolate cake shots.

"Ooh I love this song!" Zoey says, practically bouncing in her seat.

I look over my shoulder at the band and back to her. "Have you ever heard it before?" I ask her.

"Nope, but I decided I love it right now!"

Matt smiles and shakes his head at her. Zoey is definitely a little tipsy, which isn't surprising considering how much alcohol she's consumed. Female shifters don't seem to have iron stomachs like male shifters do for some reason.

Mario leans in again to talk to me when I suddenly feel something. Something *bad.*

My body flushes from head to toe, and I know I'm in deep shit as the telltale wave of my heat crashes over me.

Uh fricken oh.

Zoey's eyes go wide, and she kicks me under the table. I try to kick her back, only I kick Matt instead. He jolts in his seat a little. "Sorry," I mouth. Poor Matt, always bearing the brunt of my retaliation.

I shift in my seat, hoping that the feeling was just a fluke, but then it happens again. I stifle a groan as another wave of heat washes over me. They call it a heatwave for a reason. Female heatwaves are intense, and aside from becoming ridiculously fertile, we also literally start heating up, so that we release crazy pheromones. Which means that right now, every shifter within my vicinity will soon be able to smell it.

I look around discreetly, hoping none of the shifters besides Zoey and Matt are scenting anything. The last thing I need is an aggressive shifter fight to break out right now, which can sometimes happen. A female in heat is hard to resist, no matter the breed, and males and females have been known to fight over the promise of hooking up with a female riding her wave. We can't help it. Our animals take over.

Soon, I'll be out of my mind with lust. I need to wrap this night up now, or things will get ugly. Normally, I wouldn't even be allowed out in public if my heatwave was approaching, but I didn't think it would hit me so fast. The thought of being holed up in the sanctuary—my pack's secluded heatwave building—to ride my wave out alone, sounds awful. It's basically days or even weeks of being out of your mind with lust, and all you want is to find the nearest shifter to get jiggy with. But if you decide to ride the wave alone, then that means you have to handle business yourself and be sequestered away. Which isn't nearly as fulfilling. Dealing with your wave alone is completely unsatisfying. Toys and fingers just don't cut it. When you spend your heatwave with another shifter, their saliva and cum relieves the burning need in you, and also triples your orgasmic pleasure. Nothing is as satiating as having another shifter to do the dirty with during your wave, which is why most shifters choose to find someone to shack up with. Even humans are better than nothing.

But while riding out a heatwave with a shifter is better than doing it alone, it can leave you vulnerable, too. I've never had a steady boyfriend during one of my waves, so I've usually always picked up a human or suffered in the heat room where my animal basically whined the entire time in lusty misery.

Some females have relatively easy heatwaves, but I'm not one of them. My heatwaves are usually at least a week long, off and on. It's days of battling with my animal, coming in and out of lust-filled hazes. I can go hours or even days before hitting my second and third waves, each one just as intense, making me go full horny animal each time.

I've been known to claw at the door and beg to be let out so I can screw the first shifter I come across. They aren't Hallmark moments, I can tell you that.

I'll have to see if Mario wants to take off the edge. The first wave is always the most intense. Then I can sneak out and ride the rest of it out in solitude inside the sanctuary. It's not ideal, but a human wouldn't be able to keep up with me the entire time the way a shifter can, and none of the guys in my pack are it for me.

I would die of embarrassment if I jumped one of them. I know a lot of females make arrangements with the males in our pack, mutually deciding to enjoy the heat sex together and then go their separate ways, but I'd rather not get involved with my packmates unless it's going to be more than just sex. Shifters mate for life, and it would be too awkward if I slept with half my packmates by the time I did finally match with someone.

If Mario doesn't want to take me up on my offer tonight, I'll either have to find another human for a one-night stand, or get back onto pack land to hole up alone, but I have to hope I can get to the sanctuary before I totally lose my shit and pounce on one of my packmates. Either way, I need to leave ASAP before I start a shifter brawl here at *Dare.*

The problem is, my animal is suddenly brimming with revulsion for Mario. She already doesn't like having sex with humans during the heatwave as it is, but she's usually not so strongly averse like this. I can feel her battling inside of me, making me want to ditch him and find a shifter instead. But I'm cutting it too close now, and Mario is readily accessible, so I ignore my animal and try to trample down the repulsed feeling I'm having.

I lean closer to Mario and flash him what I hope is a flirtatious smile. "Wanna get out of here?"

He smiles back at me. "Absolutely. I'll go to the bar and settle our bill."

"Sounds good."

Mario says goodbye to Zoey and Matt, and I hop down from the stool as he makes his way to the busy bar. Based on the line, I can tell it's going to take him a bit, so I shove my phone down the front of my dress and decide to wait outside. Matt quickly excuses himself, his cheeks ruddy from the pheromones I'm starting to put out. I feel awful for subjecting him to that when he's here on a date with my best friend.

"You sure you're okay going with him?" Zoey asks me,

plugging her nose so she doesn't have to keep smelling me. "You're about to hit your first wave, and it's always crazy intense."

"It's either that or I hightail it back home and hole up in the sanctuary," I say, pressing the back of my hand against my heated brow. "But I don't even know if I'd make it in time. A motel would be closer."

Worriedly, Zoey sinks her sharp teeth into her bottom lip. "Okay. He seems nice enough. But just let him take the edge off, and then come home, okay? He can't handle more than one heatwave round."

"I know, I know," I say, leaning in to give her a kiss on the cheek. "See you...whenever this damn heatwave passes."

"Don't let your slutty animal start frisky phoning," she says, her voice nasally since she's still plugging her nostrils closed. "The last time you went into heat, you left me ten voicemails begging me to send you a shifter to sex you up."

"Bye Zoey," I say, tossing her a wave as I quickly make my way through the bar.

As I push my way through the crowd, I notice a couple of male shifters turn their noses up in the air and sniff, frowns appearing on their faces. Heart pounding, I hurry past them, not even caring when I have to elbow a few people on the way out. I need to get outside and out of scent-distance. When I make it to the exit, I push open the door and relish in the cool night air that hits my fevered skin. I instantly feel better now that I'm out in the open in the night air, and I close my eyes, taking a deep breath, trying to calm my animal and hold the heatwave at bay.

At the sound of footsteps approaching, I open my eyes and whirl around, almost colliding with someone on their way inside the bar. "Sorry," I mumble.

"My fault."

My eyes snap up at his familiar voice, and my animal immediately perks up.

Mr. Coyote Hotshot Penn Weiss takes me in, and I see recognition dawn in his eyes. "Wait. You're the girl from the bank, right? Aderyn Locke."

I take a discreet step backwards and try to smile politely. "That's right, Mr. Weiss." My voice comes out unintentionally husky. Dammit.

His eyes trail up my body, and I swear, I can feel his gaze like it's a caress against my skin. "I almost didn't recognize you with the different hair."

I reach a hand up to smooth the tangled pastel locks. I'm turning into a sweaty mess. If it weren't for the slight breeze carrying upwind, I'd be screwed right now. I start backing up again, hoping Mario will get out here soon so we can leave.

Penn notices my retreating movement and frowns at me. "What's wron—"

My back hits a hard body behind me and I turn to see the hottie from the lake—Herrick.

"Hey, Lake Lady," the dark-skinned hottie says, flashing me a smile. "I knew we'd meet again. Cool hair."

God, why did I have to run into them right *now?*

"How do you and Herrick know each other?" Penn asks me, his eyes darting between his friend and me.

I don't hear Herrick's answer, because both of their scents suddenly hit me when the direction of the wind shifts, and my animal goes *insane.* I sway on my feet like I'm drunk.

I feel Penn grab my arm to steady me, just as a *third* shifter with a man bun walks up. I'm squashed in the middle of their hottie triangle when my scent finally hits them. All three pairs of nostrils flare and their pupils dilate. They go from relaxed and friendly, to a trio of hungry predators, and I'm on the menu.

"Holy fuck, she's riding her wave," Man-Bun says with more groan than growl.

I look up at him, noting the dark brown hair swept up, and his sexy, scratchy beard. I have a sudden urge to grab his head and shove it down between my legs. I want to feel that beard all over my thighs.

Good grief. This one is coming on fast.

"I gotta go," I say, pushing past them. I can't wait for Mario. I need to leave before my animal completely takes over and I don't even have the ability to drive home anymore.

Just as I shove Penn aside, a huge wave of heat hits me

full-force, making me curl over on myself as wetness pools in my panties.

"Fuck," Herrick curses.

I feel Penn come up beside me and place a steadying hand on my upper arm, just to make sure I don't fall over with horniness. Trust me, it's a thing. "What are you doing out in public during your heat?" he asks, his tone irritated.

"I didn't know I was going into heat this fast!" I retort, yanking my arm out of his hold.

My face is on fire, and I can feel sweat dripping down the back of my neck as my temperature continues to rise. Sometimes, shifter biology sucks. This would all be great if I were mated and could reap the benefits of awesome sex and intense orgasms without having to worry about who I would hook up with. But since I'm unmated, my heatwave is unpredictable, makes me miserable with need, and can be dangerous, too.

I lift my hair up to let the night air hit my sweaty neck, but that only releases more of my scent out into the air, and I hear one of the guys groan.

"You can't leave on your own. You're too far gone," Penn points out.

"I have someone to help me," I say lamely.

"Who?" Herrick demands, looking around. "He sure as fuck shouldn't have left you out here alone. It's dangerous."

"He's inside paying," I answer, feeling my core cramping

with need. "And he's human, so he doesn't know any better," I pant out.

Herrick looks at me incredulously. *"What?* You can't go through your heat with a *human."*

Unfortunately, my animal agrees. Just the thought of letting Mario kiss me, let alone do anything else, makes me outwardly cringe. I probably would've been fine if I hadn't gotten a whiff of these three virile shifters while in my current predicament.

But now, my animal has honed in on these guys. And yeah, I can't deny the physical attraction that I'm feeling. My animal isn't the only one who wants them. They're like a three course meal, and I'm *starving.* With my biology going crazy, pushing me to mate, I don't have the ability to resist my baser instincts.

Being surrounded by this ridiculously hot trio of shifters with their delicious scents makes the most intense flood of heat rush into me. I take a deep breath through my nose, letting their scents wash over me. My eyes fully dilate and roll to the back of my head as it hits my system.

From head to toe, I turn into an inferno of need. The taut tether I was holding myself together with suddenly snaps, and my animalistic instincts completely take charge.

"Please," I beg, suddenly clutching onto Penn's arm.

"Oh, fuck."

My insides clamp down, and wetness trickles down my thighs as my eyes stay locked on Penn. I lick my lips hungrily, and I see his own eyes dilate, flashing with his animal, as he watches the movement. The next thing I know, I launch myself at him. He grunts in surprise but manages to catch me by the ass.

My legs automatically wrap around his middle as he grips me. I'm so far gone in my heatwave that I start shamelessly grinding against him. It doesn't matter that I don't really know him. It doesn't matter that I'm in a public parking lot and supposed to go home with another man. Nope, all that matters is the strong, male shifter smell wafting off of his skin, and the thing inside of his pants that I'm trying to get to.

"Fuck, she smells good," one of the other guys says. Not Penn, because I've shoved my tongue inside his mouth, taking away his ability to speak. And *damn,* he's kissing me back like he's ready to devour me. When his hands tighten against my ass, I moan. At the sound I make, he moves his head, forcing me to tilt my head to the side so he can kiss me even deeper. I'm all too happy to oblige him.

"Umm, Penn? I can see that you're enjoying this, but she's emitting some serious scent, and her panties are showing. In case you're wondering, they're green, and they say, "It ain't gonna spank itself.""

Penn groans into my mouth and promptly moves his hands to try and cover said panties like he's protecting my virtue. Snort. Pretty sure my virtue just took off her bra and flashed the camera during spring break.

As good as Penn's kisses are, I need more. I start to grip and pull at his shirt, frustrated that layers of clothing are coming between us, but my animal is in charge now, so my movements are clumsy and unsuccessful.

"That's it. We're helping her ride her wave," I hear Herrick say, and my animal practically preens with victory. "She can't go with a fucking *human* like this. Her animal will either go crazy and hurt him, or she'll be left wanting. Neither of those is acceptable."

"I agree with Herrick," Man-Bun declares. "Penn?"

Penn pulls his mouth away from mine, and I make a squawk of protest. I try to get his mouth back, but he dodges me expertly by turning his head side to side. Undeterred, I start kissing up his neck and jaw instead, and I get rewarded with a shiver.

"You okay with that, Addie?" he asks huskily, trying to get my attention.

I hear his words, but nothing registers except for this raging need inside of me. My animal doesn't understand why these three shifters aren't taking care of me, and she's getting frustrated that Penn isn't giving her what she wants—what we *both* want. I bite him on his neck hard enough to draw blood as punishment.

"Ouch!" He flinches. "Mean little thing."

Angry at him for denying me, I push away and wiggle out of his hold. As soon as my feet hit the ground, I spin and grab onto the next nearest shifter body, which happens to be Mr. Man-Bun.

"Hell yeah," he smirks.

I yank him by the beard hair to shut him up. He laughs and lifts me up, and then starts carrying me away. "Guess that's her way of saying yes," he says over his shoulder as I start nuzzling into his neck. He smells *so* good.

"Addie? What the…What's going on? Hey, Addie!"

I don't even look up at the sound of Mario's voice as Man-Bun continues to carry me off. My animal has completely dismissed him. I hear raised voices behind me, but then I'm being tossed into the back of an SUV and I don't care anymore. As soon as Man-Bun climbs in after me and shuts the door, I try to jump him, but he just chuckles and holds me back.

He presses me against the seat and then buckles me in, keeping a firm hand over my collarbone to hold me in place. I huff out in annoyance when he stays out of reach, and his brown eyes sparkle with amusement. "Patience," he chastises.

A noise close to a whine comes out of me, but it only makes him laugh. "You're gonna have to wait, beautiful."

I scowl at him, even as my hands come up to touch him anywhere I can reach.

The front doors open and Penn gets into the driver's side while Herrick hops into the passenger seat. They slam their doors shut, and Penn wastes no time peeling out of the parking lot and onto the road.

Immediately, I lean forward to try and get closer to the guys up front, forgetting about the seatbelt and Man-Bun's hold on me. When I can't reach them either, my temper rises. Unfortunately, so does my heat. I feel like I've caught on fire.

Herrick whips his head back to look at me. "She's sweltering, dude."

Penn looks at me from the rearview mirror and immediately puts my window down. I don't know if it's to let the cool air in, or to force my scent out, but it's not what I want, and my animal side doesn't understand why I'm being denied.

My frustration and need becomes so intense that tears start falling down my cheeks. Man-Bun's brown eyes widen. He slides closer to me and cups my face in his hands. "Shit. What's wrong?"

"What's happening, Lafe?" Penn asks, his tone clipped.

"I don't know, she's fucking crying!"

"It's the heatwave, dude. You're holding her back when what she needs is contact," Herrick answers.

"Well, I didn't want to take advantage and fuck her in the car!" Man-Bun, AKA Lafe, retorts.

I continue to cry, feeling the tears sizzle against my skin, and more wetness gathers between my legs as my insides clench and writhe.

"Move her over," Herrick orders.

Lafe drops his hands from my face, unbuckles me, and slides me over to the center seat. Herrick climbs to the back with us so that I'm sandwiched between them. He immediately wraps me up in his muscled arms and presses my head to his chest where I can feel his warmth and breathe in his scent. It instantly makes me feel better. Behind me, Lafe starts kneading my shoulders to get me to relax.

The touching is wonderful, but it's still not enough. Not nearly enough.

I can't talk in this state, so I just grab Herrick's hand and shove it under my dress to the spot between my thighs. He hesitates, but I swear, I'll die if he pulls away. I plead him with my eyes so he knows how much I need him to take care of me. "Don't worry, baby," he says quietly. His finger starts rubbing over my panties, and my cry turns to a pleased moan.

"Fuck, she's dripping wet," Herrick says.

The leather seat behind me squeaks from Lafe leaning forward, and his hands go into my hair. He starts stroking and pulling the strands, making me shiver. I let my back fall against Lafe's chest, and his arm goes around me to help hold me in place. Herrick moves my panties aside and then runs a finger up my soaking slit. I watch with hooded eyes as he brings the finger to his mouth and sucks it clean. "Fucking delicious."

"Drive faster, Penn," Lafe grounds out.

I can feel his erection against my back as he pulls me closer and all I want is to have it inside of me.

"Almost there," Penn replies, his voice strained. "Herrick, make her come. It'll take the edge off."

I see Herrick's white teeth flash in the dark car. "I can do that," he says, his dark eyes never leaving mine as he slowly pulls down my panties. Once they're off, he positions my legs on either side of him so that I'm wide open. "Lafe, take care of those tits for me, will you?"

Lafe immediately brings both hands under the neckline of my dress and cups my breasts. I can feel the heat of his skin through my black bra, and I arch into his touch. The second his fingers move under the cups to tease my nipples, Herrick shoves a finger inside of me. I'm so wet that it makes an embarrassing squelch, but that only seems to spur him on. He starts pumping his finger in me while his thumb plays with my clit and Lafe rolls my nipples between his fingers.

I writhe between them, grasping on whichever parts of them I can, wanting to tear off their clothes and let them mount me. When Herrick curls his finger inside of me, that's all it takes for me to come.

I clench around him and cry out, my hips lifting up in response. The orgasm is fast and furious, and ends way too quickly. Instead of taking the edge off, it only makes my body demand more.

I try to express what I need by reaching forward to grab at Herrick's erection through his jeans. He's hard and huge and he groans at my touch, but he doesn't come closer or undo his pants for me. "Soon, baby. We'll all take care of you real soon."

I hear the tires of the car scrape against gravel, and then we suddenly lurch to a stop. Car doors are opened and Herrick picks me up and passes me over to waiting arms.

Penn carries me across the yard and into a house, but I don't register any details until I'm tossed onto a bed.

When I look up, I see three ravenous coyote shifters staring back down at me. And all I can think in my heat-addled brain is *finally*.

PENN

When I first saw this shifter chick at the bank, with her cute-as-fuck blonde hair and blue eyes, I kept picturing my fist wrapped around those locks while her eyes rolled back in ecstasy. And her lips? Yeah, those lips I pictured wrapped around my dick. I'm not even that cock-crazy, but there was something about her.

She was different, surprisingly tough, and she also smelled fucking good. I'd never picked up a scent quite like hers before, but then again, at my old pack, there had only been a few kinds of shifters around, so there wasn't much diversity.

Me and the guys have been drifters for close to a year now. We've been roaming around, trying to find a new place to start over.

At first, we wanted to just be on our own for a bit, but now, we're ready to get off the road and settle into a new pack.

We got sick of the politics and the pissing contests that went on with our old pack and we wanted a change. The pack was huge, and we weren't high up enough in the hierarchy to apply for the things that should've been available to us; like a mate, private houses, or better jobs. So, we bailed.

We drove through the states, stopping at different towns along the way to check out local packs. Sometimes we even stayed in our coyote forms to hunt and run. But we haven't fit quite right with any pack yet. But this girl? Whatever pack she's a part of, I want in. I saw firsthand how she took care of that douche at the bank, and that speaks of a strong, competent alpha who actually encourages his female packmates to train, instead of keeping them stuck in the dark ages to breed and raise the pack young.

Most of the pred females back in my old pack would've just waited for a male to come along and handle things for her. But Addie? She jumped right in, no fear, and that appealed to my animal. Aside from that, the fact that she initially turned me down when I asked her out only intrigued me more, and I found myself thinking about her after the fact. I even went back to the bank to see if I could try again, only to find out that she didn't work there anymore.

So when I bumped into her tonight, it was like the universe was giving me a leg up. The fact that she's riding her wave makes it downright serendipitous and shit. I'd suggested to the guys that we go out tonight on a whim, and thank fuck, because just the thought of her going with that human while in this condition makes my teeth grind.

Addie looks up at us from my bed, her eyes wide and her pupils blown. She's flushed from head to toe, and I can feel her temperature spiking as her pores let off more of those delicious pheromones. Her scent wraps around us like a drug, making our mating instincts spiral into a frenzy.

The whole time I had to smell her while I was stuck driving, it drove me fucking crazy. I don't even want to think about how many traffic laws I broke to get us here as quickly as I did. And when she came? I nearly ran us off the road.

Now she's here, in my bed, and the scent of her heat is saturating the walls, guaranteeing that I'll be smelling her for days after, which will make my animal howl and keep me hard as a rock.

Addie starts clawing at the sheets and rubbing her thighs together like she needs to relieve the building pressure there but doesn't know how. "We got you, baby," Herrick croons.

Lafe starts stripping out of his clothes first, and Herrick and I quickly do the same. Her eyes follow us hungrily as we remove each article, and she sits up to balance on her elbows so that she can get a better view. She's so out of her mind with need and her animal is mostly in charge now, so she can't talk anymore, but she keeps making these little noises that make my cock jump.

As soon as we're all naked, she sits up on her knees and

licks her lips. I look over at the guys, and we communicate wordlessly. We've shared plenty of times before, so we know just how to take care of a female in heat.

"I get my mouth on that pussy first," Lafe declares, like the selfish bastard he is.

Herrick gets on the bed and positions himself behind her so that she can lean against his chest. As soon as he does that though, she tries moving around, making small noises of frustration when she can't get what she wants. "She wants skin-on-skin," I tell Herrick.

"Then let's give her what she wants."

He slowly unzips her little black dress and helps lift her hips before pulling it over her head in one fluid motion. As soon as he tosses it away, all three of us look down at our prize. Her gorgeous tits are on display in a black bra, but her panties are long gone from the car ride. She looks beautiful like this—wet and wanting.

Lafe makes a noise deep in his chest at the sight of her. Wasting no time, he moves forward, takes hold of her thighs, and yanks her to the edge of the bed. Then he drops to his knees and buries his head between her legs, making her cry out and fall back against Herrick's chest again.

"Her bra," I rasp, fisting my dick.

Herrick follows my order and unclasps her bra and tosses it away. My animal growls in appreciation at her bare body.

"Dude, you see how pretty these tits are?" Herrick asks,

palming them. His dark hands against her pale skin is a nice picture.

"Yeah," I tell him, her eyes locked on me. "I see."

Lafe starts lapping at her clit, and she nearly bucks off the bed. She comes quickly and fiercely, her body flushing pink, but before her orgasm can end, I tap Lafe on the shoulder. He licks her and sucks her clit into his mouth one last time, and then pulls away for me. He climbs onto the bed next to her while I move forward and line up with her center.

Gripping her thigh I pull her leg to curl around my waist. Then I aim forward, and in one brutal thrust, I slam into her. Her mouth opens in a soundless cry and she surges forward, her hands coming around to grip my ass, trying to force me deeper.

Herrick laughs, still palming her tits. "I think she likes your dick, Penn."

I look down at the "O" of her mouth as I pull out and then shove myself roughly back inside of her. "Yeah, but I think she needs more of her filled." Her face tilts up and she looks at me like she loves the words coming out of my mouth almost as much as she loves my cock inside of her.

"I agree," Herrick replies, shifting her hips to tilt up while still moving her back so that her upper body lays on his lap. He puts his finger into his mouth, getting it nice and slick, and then he reaches under her. I can tell the moment he breaches her tight little ass, because her eyes widen and her insides clench around my dick. *Fuck.*

"Lafe," I ground out.

Lafe wastes no time. He gets on his knees beside her and grips her chin, turning her head in his direction. Her already open mouth opens even wider when she sees him take hold of his dick and hold it in front of her.

She tries to move closer, but when she can't get to it, she lets out a frustrated huff that makes him chuckle. "I got you, babe."

He moves closer to her and then starts teasing her with his cock, rubbing the head around her lips and smearing his precum over them like lipstick. When her tongue darts out to taste it, all three of us groan. When she opens her mouth wide and looks up at him like she's begging, I nearly explode.

"She wants you to fuck her mouth," Herrick grates out, his finger now slowly pumping into her ass.

"Is that what you want sweetheart?" Lafe asks, running his thumb along her lower lip. He leans down and captures her mouth for a kiss, and her nails dig into my ass. Lafe pulls away, swiping the back of his arm across his mouth with a grin. "You taste good *everywhere*," he tells her.

He grabs the base of his cock and pushes inside her ready and waiting mouth, and I see the head of it push against the inside of her cheek, making her swell. The sight of her lips wrapped around Lafe's cock makes my balls squeeze.

I pump into her a couple more times and then pull out. I see her eyes strain to the side, trying to see what I'm doing, but Lafe keeps a firm hold on her jaw as he starts fucking her mouth.

"I got her ready for you," I tell Herrick with a devilish smirk.

He grins and pumps his fingers into her ass once more before pulling out and moving to lay flat on the bed. "So did I," he says salaciously.

With his help, we expertly flip her, so that she now straddles Herrick, but still faces Lafe. Lafe didn't even slip out of her mouth when we moved her, and she kept her body loose and pliant, ready to let us relocate her however we wanted. Even in the midst of her heat, it's a big deal, because it shows just how much she trusts us.

Once we get her situated, Herrick lifts her by the hips and then slowly brings her down on top of his dick, and she cries out around Lafe. Herrick is a big motherfucker. Which is why either Lafe or I always fuck the pussy first to get it ready. We would never want to hurt her, and even as slick as she is from her heat, Herrick is big enough that we need to fuck her first and make sure she's nice and loose in order for this to be as pleasurable for her as possible.

Once Herrick brings her all the way down on top of him, she sighs in relief, and his hands rub her hips in slow circles. "Good girl," he praises her. In reply, she starts moving up and down on top of him, causing him to groan and tighten his grip on her.

I move behind her, getting the front row seat of the best

show in town. She's mouth-down on Lafe and ass-up to me, while filled with Herrick's cock beneath her.

"You are so fucking sexy," I rasp, running a hand up her spine.

Goosebumps raise against her skin at the contact, and she shivers, even though her skin feels like an inferno. As if her body wants to pump us with even more desire to keep us here, I feel another wave crash over her, and her body lets off so many pheromones, that my animal nearly takes over, demanding to rut her right then. Somehow, I manage to clamp down on my animalistic instincts and stay in the driver's seat.

I can see from this viewpoint that she's absolutely dripping. Shiny wetness leaks from her pussy and trickles down her thighs, and I groan at the sight of it. I'm not one to be wasteful, so I wipe my cock all over it to lube myself up. There's more than enough. I can't wait anymore, so I line up with her puckered hole and start pushing myself in slowly.

Her whole body clenches, and she makes a loud keening noise from around Lafe's dick. I rub a hand down her arched back. "Relax, baby. You're too tight."

Herrick groans. "Her *tight* feels damn good from my position."

I chuckle, continuing to rub her gently with one hand, while with my other, I reach around and start circling her clit to relax her further. Her keening turns into small whines as I continue to push into her slowly. Her little asshole is so fucking tight, her muscles clamping around me, and I can feel every one of Herrick's slow thrusts as he moves in and out of her.

I continue pushing into her in an agonizingly slow pace. The last thing I want to do is hurt her, but goddamn, my animal wants to fuck her so badly, I can barely keep him at bay. With Herrick's help, we manage to stimulate her enough that her muscles finally relax enough to take all of me.

When I'm balls deep, my eyes roll to the back of my head and a possessive growl escapes my throat. "Fuck, *yes.*"

Herrick and I both grip her waist, and Lafe fists his hand in her rainbow hair. The three of us start moving in sync, letting her body rock between us as she moans and writhes. It feels fucking *amazing.* It must feel amazing for her, too, because I feel her come again around Herrick's cock, and he curses.

"Her pussy is like a fucking vice around my dick," he says, his fingers pinching into her skin.

"Such a good girl taking all three cocks," Lafe coos as he pets her cheek. "Look at her, she's fucking gorgeous like this, letting us fill every tight hole."

She moans again at the dirty talk, and we all feel it when yet *another* wave of heat crashes over her. Like she doesn't want our slow pace anymore, she starts pushing against me, swiveling her ass so that she can get more friction from Herrick and me.

"I hear you loud and clear, babe," I tell her. I don't need anymore hints, because her body is telling me all I need to know. I start fucking her ass hard and fast, and Herrick and Lafe match my speed.

As we move, we're frenzied, growling, rough motherfuckers. We *own* her. Use her. Dominate her. And her noises tell us how much she loves it. When her hand comes down to play with her clit, Lafe reaches down and starts to tease and flick at her nipples. Another gush of wetness leaks from her, and Herrick growls. I'm so fucking close, and my coyote is howling inside of me.

"That's right," I tell her. "Milk Herrick's cock with your pussy. I want you to come again while I come in your ass," I say, spanking her slightly. She jumps and moans at the contact.

She rubs faster against her clit, while her other hand reaches out for Lafe's balls, making him curse. "Fuck, I'm coming," he growls.

"Swallow him down, beautiful," I tell her. "Drink every last drop that he gives you," I say, as Herrick and I pump into her hard. She slurps and swallows as Lafe's cum shoots inside her mouth, his hands still gripping her hair as he jerkily thrusts.

When he slips out of her, totally spent, I take charge of her clit and start circling and pinching at it. Herrick leans up and sucks her nipple into his mouth, and that's all it takes to make her come *again.* She screams, rocking against Herrick and me, her body spasming so much that she sends both of us over the edge with her.

I groan as I shoot into her, coating her insides with my cum while Herrick does the same. *"Fuck."*

When we finish, the three of us collapse in a pile of sweat and sex.

Lafe leaves, only to return with some wet washcloths that he passes over so we can clean up. When we've wiped her and ourselves down, Herrick and I adjust our positions so that she's in the center of the bed, her body resting between Herrick's thighs.

I settle beside her so that her ass is against my crotch, while Lafe lays on her other side with his mouth against her tits. None of us can keep our hands off of her, and her limbs tangle around us, too, her hands constantly rubbing whatever parts of us that she can reach, and I fucking *love it.*

I've been with females in heat before, but it's never been like this. I've never had a female that we've been so attuned with. It's like our animals know exactly how to take care of each other. Usually, after the first wave, when a male has come inside of her, a female's heat will subside enough that her animal will take the backseat again, but it seems that Addie isn't ready for that yet.

I bury my face into her hair, breathing in the addictive scent of her. She sighs in satisfaction as I thread my fingers through her strands, while the other two run their hands gently over her skin. It seems we can't get enough of her. *I* can't get enough. I'm already getting hard again, and it's no wonder. She's even sexier now with our scent marked all over her than she was before.

Needing to feel her again, I trail my hand down to her swollen clit, only to find her hand is already there. Even though we already gave her multiple orgasms, it seems she still needs more. I chuckle darkly and give Herrick a look. Seeing where her hands are, he moves quickly, pinning her wrists to the side. "Baby, during your heat-wave, this pussy is ours," I say against her ear, nibbling at the spot just below and making her shiver.

She squirms as Lafe starts licking her nipple while I continue to work on her clit, but Herrick turns her and slips his already hardening dick into her mouth. She starts sucking and licking it like it's a goddamn chocolate shake, and moans for more. "We'll make you come again, and again, and again. Is that what you want, baby?"

She whimpers and starts grinding against my hand. I feel her cream lather my fingers as I plunge them into her. "Good girl. So wet for us."

Lafe lifts up his head from his attention on her tits, his eyes flashing with carnal hunger. "I want in her cunt this time."

I smirk at him and then look down, watching as she licks and sucks Herrick's huge dick. "What do you think, baby? Is this tight little hole ready for another dick? You want Lafe to fuck you and make you come again?"

"Yes," she says gutturally, like it's half her and half her animal speaking. It's sexy as hell. She moans and wiggles her ass against me, so I hump my hardness against her once, but then I move so that Lafe can have a turn. I move to kneel next to them while Lafe positions himself behind her.

He keeps her pressed down with her legs tucked up and

enters her slowly from behind. She moans loudly and pushes her ass further into him, making him suck in a breath. "Shit, she's so fucking *tight.*"

I palm my cock and pump it a few times, enjoying seeing them fill her at either end. When I can't stand it anymore, I scoot closer, take her hand, and move it to my cock. She immediately wraps her fingers around my girth and starts stroking me up and down.

"Squeeze harder," I tell her, and she applies the perfect amount of pressure. "Yeah, just like that, baby girl," I ground out, reaching forward to play with her tits. They're just big enough to get the perfect handful. "Play with her clit, Lafe. I want her to come again."

Lafe reaches around to take over, his thrusts growing harder, shoving her throat-deep onto Herrick's dick. When she's close to coming again, her hand on my cock stills, but I put my hand over hers and help her pump me faster. "That's it, baby. Fuck all three of these cocks like the dirty little heat whore you are. Ride that wave all over us, because we fucking *love it.*"

She screams around Herrick's dick, and he roars as he comes, too. Lafe slams into her one more time with his release, and then cum spurts out of me, gushing all over her side and dripping down to her swaying tits.

She collapses again on the bed, glowing from her orgasms, flushed from her heat, and looking absolutely fucking gorgeous with our cum soaking into her.

"We'll let you rest," I say, brushing her sweaty hair away

from her forehead. "For a bit. And then we'll take you again."

She shivers and smiles in response, and even more of her sweet cream drips out of her. I can't help but swipe a finger down and taste it. Before we can even catch our breath, she's grabbing at us again, whimpering and whining for more as she grinds against our bodies, and my coyote pushes against me hard. Yep, my animal is totally and completely addicted to her, and so am I.

Best. Fucking. Heatwave. Ever.

ADDIE

Mmmm. I had the *best* sex dream. I usually don't have those, but my heatwave must've brought it on. I'm nestled in bed, happy to stay in my cocoon of warmth as I remember the deliciousness of it all.

Three shifters at once. Too many orgasms to count. Wouldn't *that* be something. I guess Mr. Penn Weiss from the bank and Herrick from the lake really left a lasting impression on me. I feel a bit greedy for conjuring up a third shifter, though. I guess I get thirsty when I'm riding my wave.

I move to stretch, since I should probably get up, but my arms feel weird. I blink open my crusty lids, forcing myself to wake up and take stock of what's going on. My eyes swivel strangely and my mouth feels like…wait, where are my teeth…?

Oh, shit!

A loud squawk escapes me, and I fly up and out of the bed. I smack into the window, making the curtains crash down on top of me. Panicked and discombobulated, my wings flap like crazy, and I hear startled shouting erupt in the bedroom.

I try to escape the fabric, but I only get myself more tangled up. Someone finally rips the curtains away, and I look up and see all three naked guys towering over me. They stare down at me in varying degrees of surprise.

Herrick gapes. "She's…she's a…"

Lafe bursts out laughing. "Well…fuck a duck."

"Seems we already did," Penn drawls, taking in my feathered form.

Yep. I'm a duck shifter.

"Nice beak," Lafe teases.

My duck flies up at his face like she's going to snap at his nose. He makes a girly squeal and throws his arms up to try and ward her off. "Ducks are mean," Lafe whines, making Penn laugh.

My duck eyes him with warning.

"Your beak really *is* nice. I wasn't bullshitting. It's all orange and cute and shit," he says placatingly.

My duck can understand, only because I can understand, and she takes down her death glare a notch. Lafe visibly relaxes a bit. You'd think that with him being a coyote shifter, a mallard duck wouldn't wig him out so much.

I try to shift back, but my duck really likes these guys apparently, because she doesn't want to give in just yet. Plus, they're all still blissfully naked, and she seems to like the view. She starts strutting around the room, walking over their feet and ruffling her feathers. She flies up at Penn, making him flinch before she lands on his shoulder. He stays frozen underneath her, like he's scared to move.

Lafe stares at her where she's perched and lifts a finger like he wants to pet her. She snaps in the direction of his finger playfully, making him jump back and quickly drop his hand. "So…you're a duck. Is that why you woke up at the *quack* of dawn?" he teases.

Penn laughs again, but Herrick isn't amused. In fact, he looks pissed, and my duck can sense it. "You're a fucking…*duck* shifter?"

My duck squawks at the disdain dripping from his tone.

Herrick rounds on Penn. "You said you thought she was a fox or some shit!"

Penn throws up his hands, which my duck doesn't like, because it throws her off balance. She squawks and flies off of him to land on the floor at Lafe's feet. "I said I didn't know! She wouldn't tell me, remember?" Penn retorts.

"We're coyotes. We can't be screwing around with a fucking *duck!*" Herrick snaps.

My duck bristles, and my anger rises so much that I'm able to wrestle back the reins. Quick as a blink, I shift back into my human form, not caring about my own nudity. Without warning, I rear back and I punch Herrick right in the stomach. I surprise him more than anything, but he still keels over and a big "oof" escapes his stupid mouth, so I'm filled with satisfaction.

"You predators are all the same," I hiss. "Condescending assholes. You had no problem screwing me all night while I was riding my first wave, but now that you know I'm not a wolf or some other super impressive pred, now I'm suddenly not good enough for you?"

My breath heaves, and I notice Lafe's gaze zero-in on my bare breasts. I roll my eyes and spin around toward the dresser to rummage through the drawers. I pull on a pair of boxers and a huge shirt, then cross my arms over my chest. "This is *exactly* why I don't tell shifters what my animal is. Fuck you guys."

"Hold on—" Penn begins, but his voice cuts off abruptly. He tips his head up and sniffs the air, frowning as he proceeds to smell Herrick, Lafe, and himself.

"What the hell?" asks Lafe, bending away from Penn's nose.

Penn straightens up and then reaches forward and grabs hold of my wrist. As soon as he touches me, a hot, tingling sensation emits from our skin-to-skin contact. His hand makes a partial shift, with claws and golden hair suddenly erupting out of it. At the same time, tawny feathers pop out of my wrist. I squeal in surprise and we both wrench away from each other.

I gape at him as a stricken expression crosses his face. "Holy shit," he breathes, staring at me.

"What the fuck?" Herrick snaps.

Penn finally tears his eyes away from me. I already know what he's gonna say, but it isn't any easier hearing it out loud. "The mate-call has been triggered."

The guys gape at him. And then all hell breaks loose.

Penn, Lafe, and Herrick all start talking over each other in shocked denial as I continue to stand in the middle of it, my face burning with embarrassment and dismay. But there's no denying Penn's declaration. Aside from the spontaneous shifting that happens, especially with skin-to-skin contact, I can *feel* it. The new mating bond is buzzing under my skin.

Shifter females (and sometimes males) will put out a biological "mate-call" when they feel connected to another shifter on physical, emotional, and instinctual levels. And yes, it usually happens during sex. But it's always a purposeful thing. Our animals feel the need to trigger the mate-call, but then *we* can decide to go through with it or not. The mate-call is released, and the other shifter can choose to answer it by biting them, licking at the blood and sealing the bond.

Instinctively, I bring my hand up to my neck. I don't feel a mark or anything, since shifters heal too quickly, but the spot is oddly tender, and I know in my gut that it's from teeth.

Triggering the mate-call isn't common or easy, which is why shifters usually decide to trust their animal and go along with it. Some couples wait years before their animals send it out. But I barely know Penn. Surely my duck wouldn't have triggered the mate-call just because the sex was amazing?

Then again, she's never had more than one male take care of her like that at one time before. Ducks are leery of gangbangs as it is. Really. Duck gangbanging is a thing. Male ducks are freaky with their corkscrew dicks. Female ducks usually run in the other direction from multiple males. But my duck? She was *all* over these guys last night. And this morning. Many times. She's a bit of a coyote-freak, I've come to find out.

Still, my animal has *never* sent out a mate-call before. Ever. She's picky. But it looks like she did last night, although I have no memory of it. And…it looks like Penn answered it and bit me. I inwardly groan and run a hand over my face and back down to my tender neck.

"It doesn't fucking concern you," Penn snaps at Herrick, bringing me back to their current bickering. "I'm the one who answered her mate-call. So get dressed and calm the fuck down."

"The fuck it doesn't concern me," Herrick seethed. "This was just supposed to be us helping out a female last night for a good time. Now you might be tied to her indefinitely. You. A pred. Mated to a duck. That's not supposed to happen!"

I feel his words like they're a blow to my stomach, and I outwardly flinch. Seeing my reaction, Lafe steps forward. "Hey, it's okay," he soothes, placing a hand on my shoulder, his thumb brushing past the collar of the shirt I'm wearing to settle over my skin.

Feathers immediately pop out along my collarbone from the contact, and twinges of pain erupt as my shoulder and arm barely resist shifting into a wing. I look down in shock and see that Lafe's hand has turned into a paw.

I shove him off and back away with my arms raised, my feathers popping off my skin and landing on the floor. "No freaking way."

He looks from his paw to me and back again. Without skin-to-skin contact, our forms return to normal and the rest of my feathers sink back under my skin.

"...Both of us?" Lafe asks incredulously. "How can that even happen?" He steps forward again, nose raised.

He keeps sniffing at me until I swat him away. "Stop it."

He shakes his head like he's trying to clear it, but just from that one whiff, he's gone completely hard again, which is pretty difficult to miss, since he's still bare-ass naked. His dick is pointing at me like it wants the quickest directions into my vagina. I try *really* hard not to make eye contact with it, but it keeps jumping up and down like, "Pick me! Pick me!"

"Can you put pants on?" I ask, covering my eyes. He doesn't even hear me.

"We can't both have answered her mate-call," Lafe is arguing with Penn. "I mean, sure, shifters form triads and quads sometimes, but it's rare, and the mate-call never happens at the same time."

"Well, obviously, it happened. Though I don't remember answering it," Penn says, frowning at me.

"Don't look at me. I don't remember sending it out in the first place."

Shit. Were we really that high on pheromones? Yesterday I was just a single shifter, and now I have two mates? A couple of preds that I barely know? Not good. And if I made the mate-call to them, then what if…my eyes shift over nervously.

Seeing the direction of my gaze, Penn and Lafe slowly turn toward Herrick. Realization dawns on him and he shakes his head obstinately. "No," he declares. "Fuck no. I am *not* mated to a damn duck."

I went from Lake Lady, to baby, to just, *damn duck.* Ouch.

Penn nods in my direction. "See for yourself."

Herrick clamps a hand over my bicep before I can even try to back away. Almost as soon as he touches me, he wrenches away again like he's been burned. We all stare at the fur covering his palm. My stomach plummets all the way down to my toes.

"Fuck!" he yells, running a hand over his head. "Great. This is just fucking great." He rounds on me, using his tall frame to try and intimidate me. "Why would you put out the mate-call?" he demands.

"I didn't mean to," I snap. "And anyway, why would you answer it? This isn't just my fault. It takes two."

"Or four," Lafe mutters.

Herrick shoots him a scowl.

"Not helping," Penn mutters.

Herrick's disgusted display at having answered my mate-call makes me sick to my stomach. I mean, I know a duck isn't an ideal mate for a coyote. Hell, predators never mate with prey. And a duck? I can only imagine the things he's thinking right now. His old pack is legendary for its strength and its numbers. It's comprised of strong predator shifters only, and there's a big prejudice in our world against the misfits like me. Anyone who isn't a predator is looked down upon. At least, everywhere except in Pack Aberrant. I know all of this, and yet, his rejection still hurts.

"Alright, calm down," Penn says, trying to reason with Herrick. "Mate-calls can be severed if—"

My eyes widen in shock. "Whoa, whoa," I interrupt. "I know this is unexpected, but you're jumping right to severing the bond?" I can't believe what I'm hearing. It hasn't even been two hours since we had sex last, but they want to plan the very painful and emotionally distressing process of severing a mating bond? It's not like I'm excited about this either, but I wouldn't just automatically jump to severing it. If we do, there's a very good chance our animals would never form another bond again.

Without another word, I turn and march out of the room, ignoring the curses and arguing behind me. I have no car, no idea where my shoes or my phone ended up, no underwear, and I'm wearing one of these jackasses' clothes. I could kick myself right now for being so stupid.

I'm already out the door and down the driveway before Penn catches up to me. His jeans are unbuttoned and he's pulling a shirt over his head as he approaches.

"Addie, wait up," he says, grabbing my arm.

I yank out of his grasp, suppressing the partial shift that wants to erupt from his contact. "Don't touch me."

He holds up his hands in surrender. "Look, this is just really fucked up."

"You think?"

Penn sighs and brushes back his blond hair from his face. "Let me take you home. I don't want you walking."

I don't want to walk either, but I also don't want to go anywhere with this asshole. "No."

"Addie," he starts to argue.

"I said no."

He grits his teeth. "Fine. Then at least let me call someone for you."

"I'll call someone myself. Where's my stuff?" I ask instead.

"I don't know. I'll have the guys look for it," he offers, but I shake my head.

I don't want anything from them, but I remember Hugo's warning, so I swallow a spoonful of pride and hold my palm out for his phone. He digs in his pocket and passes it over to me. When I notice the time on the screen, I grimace. No way will anyone in my warehouse be up yet this early on a Saturday. I try Zoey anyway, but of course, it goes straight to voicemail. I know better than to call Aspen, because she's a ridiculously hard sleeper. That girl could sleep through an earthquake.

Out of all my packmates in the single's warehouses, theirs are the only numbers I know by heart. I wish I had my phone, because I bet I could get Stinger or one of the other enforcers at the gate, but who knows where my cell ended up after last night, and I'm not about to go back inside to go look for it. I debate for a minute, chewing on my lip, and then dial another number. He picks up on the first ring.

"Hugo," he answers.

"Hey, it's Addie."

"Addie? What's wrong?" His voice is instantly alert.

"Nothing, I just…I need a ride."

"Gimme the address."

I ask Penn and then rattle it off.

"I'll be there in ten," he promises.

We hang up, and I pass the phone back to Penn just as Lafe comes sauntering out with two coffee cups in hand. He holds one out to me, but I don't take it. He shrugs and gives it to Penn instead.

"You called a guy," Penn says, glowering at me.

I lift a brow at his tone. "Yep."

"Was that the human you were with last night?" he asks,

crossing his muscled arms and looking all kinds of pissed off.

"Wait, what?" Lafe asks, frowning. "Why would you call another guy?" I notice his knuckles are white as he clutches the handle of his coffee cup.

I look between them, surprised when I realize that they're jealous. Because I'm petty and hurt, I just shrug and turn my back on them instead of dispelling their worries. The bond that's forming between us is making their territorial and protective instincts kick into overdrive, which is even worse since they're preds, naturally inclined to fierce possessiveness. But the sting of humiliating rejection is still fresh and I don't have it in me to make them feel better.

Just remembering the way Herrick looked at me makes my stomach hurt all over again. It's not like it's the first time I've been openly mocked and scorned. I grew up feeling ashamed of who I was. I didn't belong in my own pack. Not until I left and Hugo took me in. It's why I never tell any outsiders what my animal is.

I'm no longer embarrassed by what I am, but it's ingrained in me to keep the secret of what I am so that I can keep myself and my animal safe. I've been careful to stay secluded with my packmates as my friends, while sleeping with only humans. This is the first time I've broken that rule and slept with outside shifters. It looks like I was right to be secretive.

The way Penn brought up severing our freshly forged bond makes my chest constrict, but I won't cry in front of these assholes. I've been mocked and teased and tormented my entire life about being a duck. But ever since Hugo took me in, I refuse to take anymore bullshit. So if it's driving them nuts that I called another guy, then I'll let them stew with that, because the assholes deserve it.

I may not be a fierce predator or one of the four-legged shifters that are so revered in our culture, but I won't let anyone make me feel bad about who I am anymore. I bet these guys wouldn't be considering severing the mating if I were a stupid fox. It's shifter prejudice, and I hate it. Besides, my duck is a savage thing when she wants to be. Way better than a stupid fox.

I ignore the two pissy males behind me as I continue to stand in the driveway near the street. At some point, Herrick comes out, because I hear him start to whisper-argue with the other two, but I don't listen to them.

I focus on their quiet neighborhood and the thick copse of trees behind their house. It's barely dawn, and the world is still quiet. Hugo makes it to me in record time, because in only a few more minutes of waiting, I hear his Jeep lumbering down the road long before I see him.

When he pulls up in front of us and opens his door to get out, I hear Penn hiss out a breath. "Who the hell is *he?* That's not the human from last night."

Hugo slams his door and stalks over. "I'm Hugo Hill. Alpha of Pack Aberrant," he thunders, having heard Penn's question. "Who the hell are *you?*"

All three of the guys gape. I don't blame them. Hugo is

bigger than them and you can feel the alpha power rolling off of him. He looks intimidating with the scruffy beard on his face and his beefy arms on display beneath his leather vest.

"Pack *Aberrant?*" Penn asks with shock.

"Yeah, you got a problem with that?" I challenge, crossing my arms. Coyote or not, I will go duck-shit crazy on his ass if he says one thing against my pack.

Hugo steps between the guys and me. He has his scary alpha face on as he looks them over. He snorts, unimpressed, and then turns around to give them his back. It's kind of a dick move, because it lets them know that he doesn't consider them as any kind of threat, even though there are three of them and one of him. But he's an alpha, and he's badass like that. Also, I'm pretty sure he could easily kick their asses.

"Hey, Alpha."

"You okay, kid?" he asks, his voice softer as he looks me up and down. He notes my lack of shoes and my borrowed attire, and his scowl deepens. He sniffs the air and goes still, his eyes widening in surprise. "You're in heat and you're *mated?*"

I grimace and Hugo whirls back around on the guys. "What in hellhound's ballsack is going on? Did you take advantage of her?"

The guys become visibly cowed. Even Herrick. Hugo may be older, but I have no doubt he could do some serious damage to them. I take pity on them and lightly touch

Hugo's arm. "I hit my heatwave last night. I pretty much jumped them in the parking lot," I confess. "I didn't mean to put out the mate-call, and they didn't mean to answer it. It just happened."

"They?" he repeats incredulously. "You mean you're mated with all of them?"

"Umm...Yeah…"

"Are you telling me that you were out in *public* when your heatwave came on last night?" he asks, his expression turning stony.

I look down, giving myself away.

Hugo rubs a hand down his face. "Fuckin' balls. You know the rules, Addie. You should've been sequestered away long before it hit, either with someone, or alone to ride it out."

"I didn't know it was gonna hit me so fast," I say, feeling embarrassment color my cheeks.

"And now you have three assholes for mates," he points out, jerking a thumb over his shoulder at them.

The guys are smart enough not to comment.

"Yeah. Hindsight."

He sighs. "I can't bring you back to the compound with you still riding your wave. The males won't be able to control themselves. Plus, the Rockhead Pack representatives are coming to meet with me today about our recent issues. I won't risk them seeing *or* scenting you."

My head whips up to look at him and fear grabs me. "Shit. They're coming to our compound?"

He nods gravely, and I can see the sympathy in his eyes. Hugo is like a father to me. He's the only person I've ever told about my childhood and my family, so he knows the implications of me being in the proximity of anyone from Pack Rockhead.

All three of the guys must pick up on my fear, because they go still. Damn mate bond. "What's going on, Addie?" Penn asks.

I ignore him and chew on my fingernail. "Okay. I'll stay at a motel tonight."

"I don't know, Addie. I don't like you staying alone outside of pack land," Hugo says with a frown.

I open my mouth to tell him that I'll be fine, but Penn butts in. "No, you should stay here, with us. Your *mates*."

I curl my lip in disgust and shift around Hugo to see him. "Oh, *now* you want to call me your mate? What happened to severing the bond?"

Hugo rears back and whirls around to face them again. "Wait…let me get this straight," he says, his voice low and threatening as he curls his lip at them. "The three of you peanut pricks took advantage of my pack member during her heatwave, answered her mate-call, and then threatened to sever the bond as soon as she got out of your bed? Is that what you're fuckin' telling me?"

Lafe swallows and Penn grows visibly paler. Even Herrick manages to look contrite.

"Get in the car, kid," Hugo tells me in a deathly quiet tone, his dark gaze still locked on the guys. "I need to have a little chat with these boys, here."

I turn away to follow my alpha's instructions. Just as I open the door to his Jeep, I hear Hugo's furious voice. "So, you're a trio of hotshot preds, thinking you can look down on my girl because you've got canines and hairy dicks?"

I don't hear the rest, because I close the door behind me after I slide into the Jeep. I stare straight ahead and try to push down the awful feeling of separation that's already brimming inside of me.

I'm barely ten feet away, but my animal is going nuts. The bond may be brand new, but they're my mates, so being apart from them is physically painful. Newly bonded shifters aren't supposed to separate. Aside from that, I'm still riding my heatwave. Since I've been sated all night and for part of the morning, I'll get a reprieve, but that could last anywhere from a couple of hours, to a couple of days. There's no way of knowing, and then it will hit me all over again. Hopefully, it won't be as strong as my first wave was.

A minute later, Hugo stalks to the Jeep, gets in, and peels out onto the street. I don't look out the window for a last glance at the guys. I just keep my face pointed straight forward, avoiding them completely.

It's not until the house is out of sight that Hugo speaks up. "How bad is it, kid?"

I didn't even realize I was curling over onto myself, trying to stave off the separation pain that's stabbing into my chest. I force myself to sit back, breathing out between my teeth. "I'm fine."

He snorts. "Like hell you are. If they weren't such assholes, I'd tell you to stay with them."

"One thing about being a misfit. You know when you're not wanted."

He says nothing, but he tightens his grip on the steering wheel. I change the subject, hoping to distract myself from the pain. "So. Pack Rockhead. Do you think they'll try anything?"

"Don't know. They won't outright challenge us, though. It's not their style. Not even when you defected and joined us. They prefer to do that shady, sneaky shit. Still, I don't want you anywhere near them. It's bad enough that you see them in town sometimes."

I shrug. "They talk shit, but they're too scared of you to actually hurt me."

"Good," he says with a vicious smile on his face. "They should be."

I clear my throat. "Is my stepdad coming?" I ask, staring down at my lap.

Hugo shakes his head. "I don't know."

Silence hangs between us as I turn to look out the window. It's been ten years, and the memories of my childhood are still as fresh as ever. The first time I shifted,

I was two. My parents are wolves. Well, my mom and *step*dad, anyway.

Turns out, my mother had an affair with a drifter. She didn't even get his name, let alone what kind of animal he was. To say that it was a surprise when I shifted into a duckling is putting it mildly. I was tormented from then on out, even by my parents. My stepdad hated me on sight, once he realized I wasn't his. My mother blamed me for letting the duck out of the bag, so to speak.

As far as Pack Rockhead…yeah, I wasn't welcome. I had two options once I came of age. Fight, or leave. I was a fifteen-year-old girl who would've had to go against twenty and thirty-something seasoned shifters. There was no choice.

Pack Rockhead was a pred-only pack. Being the only prey animal in that environment had been brutal. No friends, no real sense of family or love. I was shunned and hated, kept secret like a dust bunny pushed under a rug when company came over. I would've most definitely been killed if I had tried to fight the pack for status to stay. So I left.

Fifteen years old, broke, and completely alone, I didn't get very far. I stayed in a few abandoned places around town, wondering where I was going to go and scared out of my mind that I'd be beaten up, kidnapped, or worse. Some of my old packmates that I'd grown up with were still gunning for me, like Drag and Jordy.

I had no idea why they hated me so much, but the day I defected from the pack and chose exile, I believed them when they said that they'd track me down. Which is why I couldn't stay in one place more than a single night. Wolves had an excellent sense of smell, so I didn't want to risk it.

At least while I was still a part of the pack they always stopped short of killing me, since that was against the rules, and it would've pissed off Alpha Rourn for the mess it would've made. As meager as that protection was, I missed it sorely once I defected. There were no laws to protect rogue shifters without a pack, so I had to be careful. I covered my tracks.

I carried around a spray bottle of ammonia to cover up my smell whenever I stayed somewhere, and I made sure to spray it on my clothes too, just in case. It smelled awful, but it covered up my scent, and that was what mattered. I had to stay in whatever place I could find, since I didn't have any money to rent a room, and no one would hire a teenage girl who looked like she'd swallowed more pride than actual meals.

Call me naive, but I kept thinking that my mother would come to her senses, realize how much she missed me, and bring me back home. But that never happened.

After the third week, I'd made up my mind to try hitch-hiking out of town, and leave everything behind me to start over somewhere new. In fact, I was on my way to do just that. With my backpack hanging over my shoulder, everything I owned inside, I left the empty barn shed I'd been sleeping in and started making my way toward the gas station in town where I knew I'd have a better shot of asking for a ride.

Luck must've been in a good mood that morning, because while I was leaning against the outside wall of the gas station, watching for truckers, who should walk up but Hugo. He took one look at me, and he just knew. It took some convincing on his part—I was pretty skittish—but when he bought me a gas station hot dog and promised that his pack accepted shifter misfits like me, I was pretty much sold. Hugo had just purchased land nearby, so he took me in and has been like a father to me ever since. I've found a family with Pack Aberrant, but the proximity of my old pack means that I've never really escaped them.

"It'll be alright, kid," Hugo says, as if he's able to sense the direction of my thoughts.

I glance over at him, the corner of my mouth tipping up. "You're a good alpha, you know that?"

He grunts under his breath. "Don't be gettin' all sappy and shit."

I laugh and push all of those thoughts away. "Did you see those guys' faces? You totally freaked them out."

Hugo chuckles. "Cocky little fucks."

I nod, while still pretending like I'm not a total mess over the strained mating bond. It hurts like a bitch, and my animal is unsettled, pacing inside of me and wanting to reunite with them. "Preds are all the same," I say with a sigh. "Well, except you," I tease the jaguar shifter.

He chuckles and shakes his head, but then the humor drops from his face. "You could've been hurt, kid. Or you could've caused a mob being out in public like that. That wasn't smart. You know we always play smart."

I blow out a breath. "I know. I messed up."

"Wish I could take you home, but it just isn't safe."

"I'll be okay at the motel. Hopefully it doesn't last too long."

"You know the drill when you stay off pack land while riding your wave."

I nod. "Rent a room away from others and a corner unit if possible. Request cleaning supplies to spray the edges of the door. Stuff cloth under the door jamb and windows if there are gaps, and don't leave the room under any circumstances."

"You got it."

It might sound dramatic, but a female riding her wave is no joke. I've heard that some shifters with a strong sense of smell can pick up the scent of a female in heat from up to a mile away. The only reason Hugo isn't affected by me is because he's the alpha leader of the pack, which means massive power and control.

He also has a specific connection with all of his pack-mates, since we all went through the pack joining ritual when we became a part of Aberrant, which included offering him our blood. Hugo can sense when one of his pack is mortally injured or dies. His animal also has total control over our animals.

"Don't worry about me, Alpha," I tell him, trying to alleviate the frown between his brows.

"Kid, you're my pack. I'll always worry about you, just like I worry about everyone else."

He really is a great alpha. It always baffles me that he doesn't have any kids of his own, because in shifter years, he's still in his prime, and he'd be an excellent father.

I look at him curiously. "How come you've never mated, Hugo? I bet lots of females try to catch your fancy."

He raises a bushy brow and gives me side-eye. "What did I tell you about that sappy shit?"

I laugh and hold up my hands in surrender. "Sorry. Maybe this whole newly-formed bond thing is screwing with my head," I say, rubbing at the aching spot in my chest.

He notices my movement and frowns. "Those assholes will come to their senses and realize they'd be fuckin' *lucky* to keep you as a mate."

I scoff. "Yeah, I doubt that. They're coyotes. I'm a duck. I'm sure you can guess how that went over once they found out what kind of animal sent out a mate-call to them."

He grunts something with a pissed off look on his face just as he turns off the highway and pulls up to a motel with a sign that blinks, "Vacancy."

Hugo parks in front and pulls out his wallet and hands me a stack of cash. "Here. Get inside and stay inside. You get hungry, you order in. I'll send Zoey over with clothes when it's safe. As soon as those Pack Rockhead assholes leave, I'll let you know."

"Thanks, Alpha," I say as I hop out of the Jeep.

"Yeah, yeah. Play smart. Stay inside or I'll ground your ass to the compound and make you do crop duty."

I grimace. The thought of handling a shovel does not sound like a good time. "No need to resort to nasty threats. I'll be smart."

"Good. Now get your ass inside, kid. I have to get back or I'd walk you in myself."

"No worries. Get back and show those Pack Rockhead jerks who's boss."

"That's the plan."

I wave as he pulls away, and then I go inside to the motel lobby to secure myself a room. The front desk clerk looks like he's about sixteen years old, with acne on his face and a cell phone glued to his hand. As soon as he sees me walk in, he blanches. Probably because of my current state of undress. He fumbles on his phone, typing away, but drops it by the time I make it up to the counter.

"Hi. Can I get a room?"

He stutters and starts shuffling papers around nervously. "Yeah, let me just…" He gives me a sheepish look. "Sorry, computer's down. It'll just be a few minutes."

I shrug and meander around the lobby as I wait. All I want to do is soak in a bathtub and ride out the rest of my wave in peace. With a vibrator. Unfortunately, I don't have one of those stuffed in my borrowed boxers, so my hand is going to have to do.

It takes forever for the kid to finally check me into a room. Way longer than I want to be waiting in the condition I'm in. At least no one else has come in and seen me like this.

I'm just finishing up paying with Hugo's cash and getting my room key when I hear, "Addie?"

I whirl around in surprise and see the last person I want to run into right now. My jilted date, Mario Perez.

9

ADDIE

Mario saunters over to me as I snatch up the keycard and turn to face him. Am I grimacing? Yep, I'm grimacing. What should I do with my hands? Should I wave? Offer him a fist bump?

Crap. I just saluted him.

"Hey, Mario," I say, trying to sound nonchalant to cover up the weird salute thing, but really, there's no coming back from that.

He stops in front of me, and his eyes take in my bare feet, loose boxers, huge t-shirt with no bra, and my tangled hair, which looks like I tried to build a nest in it. I can feel caked-on eye makeup stuck to my lashes too, so I probably have raccoon eyes. To sum it up, I look awesome. He, on the other hand, doesn't look like a hobo. He's showered and dressed and everything. I still have sex juices stuck to me. Kill me now.

"Are you okay? What the hell happened last night?" he asks me with a frown.

Hmm…what's the best way to explain why I ditched him —after he paid for my dinner and drinks—to jump three strangers in the parking lot and have an animalistic orgy…?

"I…umm…"

Yeah, I got nothin'.

"Are you with those guys?" he asks, sounding hurt.

"No," I answer automatically, shaking my head. "Last night… Last night was a big fat mistake. Three *really big,* fat mistakes," I amend. Then I grimace again, because now it sounds like I'm calling their dicks big. Which they were, but still. It's not polite conversation. Plus, I think I just made it obvious that I ditched him not just for one of the guys, but for all three. Again, not polite conversation.

Mario brushes his hair back and blows out a breath. I shuffle my feet awkwardly, and, ew. I just realized how gross this lobby carpet is on my bare feet. Pretty sure my feet pores need to be cleansed after this. I wonder if that raw potato trick works…?

"Listen," he says, breaking me out of my train of thought. "Why don't we go to breakfast and talk?"

My blonde brows shoot up in surprise. Mario saw me with my limbs wrapped around Penn last night as I sucked his face off. He saw me get into the back of someone else's SUV and take off, after I'd basically told him I would go home with him. And now, he's seeing the evidence of my walk of shame, but he still wants to get together to talk to me? I feel like such an asshole. He's way too nice for me.

"Umm, sure. But, maybe not...right now," I say, cringing at my appearance again. "How about this weekend?"

He seems to remember my sticky appearance and quickly nods. "Sounds good. Let me walk you to your room at least."

Aww. What a cutie patootie.

"Okie dokie."

We make our way outside and I follow the signs to find my room number. This motel is only two levels and not very big, so it's not too far of a walk. Which is fortunate, since the sidewalk is also pretty gross. As I sidestep a questionable brown stain, a used condom, and then a crushed lollipop on the ground, I find I have a newfound appreciation for shoes.

The entire motel is pretty run down, but I can't fault Hugo for taking me here. The other hotels in town are always filled with human tourists, and just in case something were to go wrong with me, well, it's better that it happen in a place like this away from eyes that have enough money to ask questions. The people who stay in places like this know enough to look the other way. It's a side effect of down-on-your-luck survival.

"I'm this way," I tell Mario, feeling slightly nervous as he walks me. My mate bond is also giving me angry twinges deep in my chest at being with a male that isn't my mate. I scratch the spot, urging it to go away.

"What are you doing here, anyway?" I ask. "I thought you lived in town."

"Oh. Umm…"

I glance over at him, my curiosity piquing, but before he can answer, we round the corner of the building, and something suddenly knocks against my throat and my body is slammed hard into the wall.

The back of my head cracks against the hard stucco, making me see stars. When I blink away the fuzziness, I see Mario and another guy in front of me. Mario has his forearm pressed against my windpipe and an ugly gleam in his eye. Okay, so he's definitely *not* a cutie patootie who's too nice for me, then. I read that one totally wrong.

I try to knee him in his groin, but the other guy kicks my kneecap before I can, sending sparks of pain through me, and Mario shoves his hips against mine to stop me from being able to move again. He loosens his hold on my throat just enough for me to take in a breath, and I gulp down oxygen as quickly as I can, trying to breathe through the pain. I try to scream to draw attention too, but Mario shoves his hand over my mouth before I can get enough sound out.

"Aderyn Locke," the other guy sneers.

My wide eyes move over to the voice, and with a jolt, I recognize him instantly. Drag, one of the shifters from

Pack Rockhead, and one of my biggest childhood tormentors.

He grabs both of my wrists and wrenches them painfully to the side. He's huge—big enough to compare to Hugo, but where Hugo is naturally brawny and strong, Drag just looks like he's had a case of too many beers. He's bald, and the top of his head shines like a bowling ball. I watch as his pupils immediately dilate from the heatwave pheromones I'm still giving off. They're not nearly as strong right now while my heat is in limbo, but it's only a matter of time before it gets stronger again. I definitely do *not* want to be around Drag when that happens.

"So, you're the bitch that got our guys arrested," Drag says, making me frown in confusion. "Should've fuckin' known."

Mario nods. "Yep, I made sure she was the right bank teller. It's her."

I try to curse him out, but his sweaty palm is still covering my mouth.

Drag chuckles darkly. "Course it was you," he says to me. "You always were a little cunt."

Anger, embarrassment, and indignation swirls inside of me. So, Mario singled me out at the gamer club because of what happened at the bank robbery, and not because he liked me? Well, that's just…disappointing. Talk about a blow to the ego. And apparently, he's working for Pack Rockhead. My ex-pack and all around nemesis. Awesome.

Mario didn't just *happen* to be here at the motel. He

must've tracked me somehow and approached me as soon as he saw I was alone, and then lured me out, distracting me enough that I didn't sense Drag before I was attacked.

"You cost us a lot of money," Drag sneers. "And you got our humans arrested."

Well, that's interesting. I've never heard of Pack Rockhead hiring humans to do work for them before. Hugo will need to know about this. But if I have any hope of telling him, then I need to get away from Drag and Mario.

Luckily, when I joined Pack Aberrant, Hugo made it mandatory to train in self-defense. Even though it was difficult and I gave my fair share of grumbles and complaints, I'm thankful that he did it. As a scrawny teenage girl who felt like she didn't belong, self-defense training was how I first bonded to Hugo and a few other of my packmates.

So in this moment, I'm glad for that training, because I don't feel totally helpless right now, but even so, I know that this situation isn't good. I'm outnumbered, they're stronger than me, and I'm in a terrible position pinned against the wall. Plus, Drag can smell that I'm going to be riding my wave soon, which will automatically put him in a rut and make him more aggressive.

"Go get the car," Drag orders.

Mario quickly drops his hold on me and runs off to do Drag's bidding. I try to get away, but Drag is too quick, and steps into me as soon as Mario pulls away. With his body crushing mine, he makes my back and head dig painfully into the wall. Then he yanks my hands forward and presses them against his groin. I try to move away, but his grip is too strong. He forces me to touch his growing erection, no matter how hard I try to pull away.

"I'm kinda glad it's you who ruined our payday. You won't be able to run away from me now," he says, leaning in to sniff my hair. "Newly mated, huh? Well, that can be undone," he says with an evil smirk. "Remember all the fun we used to have as kids? I can't wait to play with you some more."

My stomach roils and my mating bond protests. I try to pretend that his words don't affect me, but as I feel his erection grow harder under my hands, I'm filled with revulsion and dread. He leans in and licks my neck, and bile rises in my throat. "Let me go!" I thrash against him, trying to get my hands off of him, but he's strong, and he makes sure to step on my bare toes with his boots, making my toes curl in pain.

I know that panicking won't help me, so I force myself to stop thrashing and take a deep breath. When I'm calm again, he smirks at me. "Always a prey at heart."

Ignoring his taunt, I try to turn things around back on him. "So, Pack Rockhead is hiring humans to rob banks now? You're that desperate for cash? You guys are pathetic," I spit.

He doesn't take the bait. "Oh, yeah. I'm gonna have a good time with you, little freak."

Over my dead body will I let that happen. But, yeah, I'd be lying if I said I wasn't feeling panicked right about now. Unfortunately, my animal side is panicking, too. It's one

of my "defects," as my old pack used to call it. Most
shifters can easily shift into their animals when they're
feeling threatened.

But for me, my animal side usually retreats further inside
of me and refuses to come out when she's feeling vulnerable. Fight or flight response. And, yeah, she's a duck, so
her instinct is flight. I can't blame her. But mine? Mine is
to fight a motherfucker. I can thank Hugo for that, too.

When Drag smells me again and tries to thrust into my
hand, I lose it. I bring my head back and then slam my
skull against his nose as hard as I can. He yowls in pain
and grips his face, but in his shock and pain, he backs
away from me slightly. It's all I need.

I bring my leg up and knee him as hard as I can in the
balls, erection be damned. When he bends over to clutch
his groin, I lift up the front of his shirt, pulling it up and
over his head and cut off his view. Then I dance back and
kick him in the back of the kneecaps as hard as I can. He
falls down to the ground, unable to catch himself, and I
take off.

I run as fast as I can toward the parking lot when I
remember that Mario is still around. While I'm sure I can
take him, I don't want to stick around for Drag to catch
up with me. I surprised him this time, but I won't get so
lucky again, and I can't overpower both of them at the
same time. I start to double back toward the lobby when a
motorcycle screeches to a stop in front of me, nearly
taking off my toes.

"Get on!"

I can't see his face through the visor of his helmet, but I recognize Lafe's voice and scent immediately. I jump onto the back of his bike and wrap my arms around him. As soon as I do, he peels out of the parking lot, cutting off a white SUV. Mario is behind the wheel and he easily spots me, since I have no helmet on.

"Shit."

I watch as Mario immediately spins the wheel around to follow us out onto the street, and I lean up to yell close to Lafe's ear. "He's following us!"

Lafe moves one of his hands off the handlebar and yanks his helmet off, passing it back to me. My hair is blowing wildly around my face, but I manage to shove the helmet over my head with one hand. As soon as both of my arms are wrapped around him again, he picks up the speed and starts flying down the street so fast that a scream tears out of my throat.

We weave in and out of cars, passing their blurred figures faster than I can focus on them. My toes and legs become frozen in a matter of seconds, and the wind keeps blowing my shirt up, no doubt flashing people as we speed by, but I keep my death grip on Lafe and just hope that I don't fall off.

I always used to think that motorcycles were awesome, but no one ever tells you that they're freaking scary. I look back to see if Mario is still following us on the busy highway, but he's nowhere in sight. I let out a huge sigh of relief, but I don't let up on my hold, and I'm grateful that Lafe doesn't try to get me to loosen up. I'm way too scared for that, and my heart pounds the entire time.

He drives around on the highway for awhile, and then starts taking backstreets for a good hour before doubling back and heading to his house. When he finally pulls into his driveway and parks the motorcycle inside his garage, my body feels completely numb and raw from being wind-whipped the entire time.

Lafe hops off and then reaches out to take my hand. My legs are shaky and unstable as I lift my leg over, so he helps steady me for a minute before reaching over and lifting the helmet off of my head. I thought my hair was a tangled mess before, but now I look like I stuck my finger in an electrical socket.

"First time on a bike?" he smirks.

I rub my arms, trying to get the feeling back into them. "How could you tell?"

"Well, it was somewhere between the death grip and the shrieking."

I cross my arms. "I do not shriek."

His smile widens. "Sure you don't."

He runs his hands up through his long hair and re-ties it in his signature man bun, and I'm annoyed at how good it looks. He frowns when he catches sign of the goosebumps all over my skin. "Sorry. I should've given you my jacket," he says sheepishly.

"I think that would've been a bit difficult while you were

going a thousand miles per hour and taking ninety degree turns," I reply with a smirk. I like Lafe, and honestly, his reaction to me and my duck this morning wasn't bad. He wasn't disgusted like Herrick and he didn't act like I was an inconvenience like Penn did. Out of all of them, I felt like me being a duck didn't matter so much to Lafe. But maybe that's just hopeful thinking.

"Come inside. You can use the bathroom to shower and get warmed up. Then you can call your alpha."

He locks up the garage and then leads me inside the house. As soon as we cross the threshold, I notice how quiet it is. "Where are Penn and Herrick?"

"Herrick took off right after you left. Penn did, too."

"Herrick was a dick." There, I said it.

Lafe looks over at me in surprise, but he doesn't dispute what I said. "Yep," he says, agreeing easily. "So. A duck. I've never come across a duck shifter before."

"Like most prey, there aren't many of us left," I reply.

He hums under his breath as he leads me down the hall-way. "Hey, you wanna relax and watch some duck-umen-taries later?"

I punch him lightly on the arm, which only hurts my hand and makes him laugh harder. "Sorry. Bird puns really quack me up."

I roll my eyes. "You're annoying."

"Oh, come on, you know you want to tell me to duck off."

I can't stop the smile that spreads across my face. I know that Lafe is mostly doing this to help relax me, and I appreciate it immensely.

"Wanna play a round of duck duck coyote?" He wags his brows.

"Shouldn't it be coyote coyote coyote duck?"

"Now you're thinking," he says, tapping his temple with a grin. "Okay, how about this—how do you change a duck's tires?"

"Did you look these up on the internet?"

"With a quacker jack," he says, ignoring my question. "Hey, sexy. Wanna flock?"

I laugh and slap his side. "Okay, okay. Stop."

"Sure thing, duckling," he says with a mischievous wink.

Lafe is so easy to be around, that I find myself relaxing. Thank goodness he showed up when he did. I'm not sure what would've happened otherwise. I don't even want to think about everything right now, but the fact that Pack Rockhead is out to get me isn't good. In their eyes, I cost them their payday, and I know they aren't going to let that go. But for now, I'm safe, and my mate bond isn't hurting anymore with Lafe so close.

When we reach the end of the hallway, Lafe opens the door to his bedroom and steps aside to let me in first. It's smaller than the bedroom we had sexy times in, but it suits him. There are old eighties rock band posters framed on the walls and a black bedspread messed up from sleep on top of the bed. But my eyes hone in on the guitar propped in the corner. "You ride a motorcycle *and* play guitar? Geez Louise. What a stud you are."

He laughs and scratches the brown scruff on his jaw. "I'm pretty shit at it to be honest."

I smile at his candor. "That's okay. I tried learning the violin when I was sixteen and ended up slamming it against the concrete driveway. I'd saved up for that damn thing for five months, too."

He nods to the guitar. "That's my third one. I drove over the first and chucked the other into a river."

I tip my head back and laugh, and his own low laughter joins mine. It feels good to laugh with him, and it dispels some of the awkwardness. After all, I don't really know Lafe at all. Heck, the first time I met him was last night, and I jumped him before I even got his name. But damn, I'm just as attracted to him now as I was then.

Lafe is hot, funny, and easy to be around. He also knows how to handle the stick in his pants. No wonder my duck wanted to claim him.

When our laughter tapers off, I let out a long breath, like I can exhale all of the tension that happened back at the motel. "Hey, thanks for saving my ass back there," I tell him seriously.

"Nah, I didn't save your ass. I was just your getaway. But I do want to know what the hell happened back there. I was about to park when I saw you sprinting across the parking lot. It looked like you needed to get out of there fast."

"I did," I confess.

His face grows worried. "Who was that following us? What happened, Addie?"

"Mind if I borrow your phone?" I hedge.

He digs into his pocket and passes it over. Knowing that Zoey will be awake by now, I shoot her a quick text with Lafe's address.

If I were to call Hugo, he probably wouldn't answer because he's supposed to be meeting with Pack Rockhead. And if he *did* answer while they were still there...well, I have a feeling that the meeting wouldn't go so well. I need to wait until the meeting ends so that he doesn't freak out and start a pack war. I don't want him to get pissed on my behalf and do something he'd later regret. Hugo is protective of me, maybe more than some of the others, but I refuse to let that hinder him when he's keeping our pack safe.

I don't know what Pack Rockhead is up to, but it's nothing good. They outnumber us and have much stronger animals than us, too, so like Hugo always says, we have to play smart.

"Did you track me to the motel?" I ask Lafe as I finish texting Zoey and pass the phone back to him.

He rubs the back of his neck like he's embarrassed. "Umm, yeah."

"How did you find me? You couldn't have scented me."

"I followed behind your alpha's car. I made sure to keep a good distance between us, and people don't usually notice motorcycles as much. When I saw him drop you off at the motel, I turned around to head home. I was about half way there when I got a bad feeling and decided to go back. That's when I saw you running in the lot."

I study him. "Why? Why follow me in the first place?"

He shrugs. "I couldn't help it. My animal," he explains. "I needed to make sure you were okay. And separating hurt more than I expected, to be honest," he says, tapping at a spot on his chest. The same spot where my own mate bond had ached.

I grimace a little because regardless of how the others feel about me, I know that they must be having a hard time with the separation too. I've heard that it's even worse for the males, because their protective instincts kick in. And not only is it caused by the mate-call, but they soaked in all my pheromones last night as I rode my first wave, so I've put them into a rut. Their animals probably went nuts when I left.

I tug on a strand of my hair. "I'm sorry for the whole surprise mate-call thing. And for putting you in a rut."

He reaches forward and takes the hair out of my hand so I stop pulling on it, and tucks it behind my ear. It's such a sweet and intimate gesture that my breath catches. "Believe me, I don't mind," he says quietly, surprising me.

"You don't mind being suddenly mated to a stranger?"

"You're not a stranger," he says, taking a step forward so that we're only inches apart. Having him this close makes my heart thump hard against my chest and the mate bond starts humming under my skin.

I clear my throat and try to maintain a composed façade. "Still, it was irresponsible of me to be out in public when I knew my heat was coming. And as for the accidental mate-call that I put out…" I grimace. "What if you'd had a girlfriend or something? You didn't ask for this. I put you in a bad position."

"Oh, we were in all kinds of *positions,*" he says devilishly, his eyes flashing with lust as he reaches out to grip my hips and pull me flush against him. "But like I said, I'm not complaining." He leans in to scrape his scratchy beard against my jaw. The skin-to-skin contact instantly stimulates my heatwave, and I have to suppress the urge to shift.

I shiver and my eyes flutter closed. "I'm gross."

His tongue darts out to lick the sensitive spot below my ear. "No, you're not."

"I'm covered in sex juices." My argument doesn't do much since I also tilt my head to the side to give him better access to my neck.

"You're marked with our scent. With *my* scent. Our cum and sweat and saliva is soaked into your skin, mixed with your heat pheromones, and it's the sexiest fucking thing in the world. Not to mention your mate-call is like a drug all on its own. I have to touch you. I have to be *in* you again," he adds, nipping at my neck.

His erotic words make me whimper. His touch is like a drug that I'm quickly learning to crave. Lafe's hands move from my hips to grip my ass, and I'm reminded once again that I have no panties on when wetness starts to gather between my thighs. As if he can sense it, he trails a finger up the leg of the boxer shorts and seeks out my slick heat. He growls appreciatively at what he finds there, and my skin grows fevered.

"People weren't joking about having a mate during heat," I say, trying to laugh off the sensations that he's filling me with, but failing miserably when his finger starts teasing my clit. "Holy guacamole," I breathe, making him chuckle.

"You're the sexiest damn surprise mate I've ever seen," he says in my ear.

I tip my chin up, because I need to feel his lips on mine. He brings a hand up to cradle my jaw, but before he can follow through and press his lips on mine, we hear the front door open and slam shut, making me jump back.

Lafe shakes his head. "Those assholes have the worst timing."

"I can be quiet," I whisper, not wanting to stop yet. His brown eyes flash with mischievous hunger, as mine dart toward the still open door.

"How about we make it a game? You try to be quiet while I try to make you scream?"

I nod enthusiastically, because that seems like a *very* good game. "Okie dokie. Sounds like a plan."

He chuckles and moves to grip my hips again, but then

we're interrupted again when we hear voices. First, it's Herrick's low timbre, but then I hear something that makes all of the lust drain right out of me.

Giggling. A *female* giggling.

My eyes flash with uncontrollable rage and the next thing I know, I've shifted.

My duck takes over, and she is a form of feathered fucking fury.

She flies out of Lafe's bedroom faster than he can grab her. She waddles her tawny ass down the hallway before I can even try to retake control. Side effect of the heatwave and the answered mate-call—it kinda makes us lose our shit when we think our territory is being threatened. And yeah, until the bonds are severed, the guys are *my* territory. So another female giggling with Herrick? Yeah, my duck is ready to beak a bitch.

When my duck gets to the living room, I'm forced to watch from the sidelines out of her eyes, as we both take in the scene. What we see makes fury ignite to a flame that really crisps my duck's feathers.

Herrick is on the couch, and there's a woman straddling his lap and looking like she's trying to suck his face off. And he's kissing her right back.

Oh *hell* no.

10

ADDIE

My duck snaps.

One second, my duck is in the doorway, and the next, she's quacking like crazy and launching at the woman whose tongue is slathering up Herrick's face like he's her favorite flavored popsicle.

When my duck flaps around her head, the woman flinches back and starts screaming all high-pitched and girly. Unimpressed, my duck flies up to her head and gets tangled in her blonde hair, and Blondie goes ballistic.

Blondie jumps up from Herrick's lap and starts running around the room in circles, which that doesn't actually do anything. My duck is a pro at holding on. She snaps her beak, aiming for the woman's nose, feeling victorious when she manages to get a small nip at it. My duck *always* goes for the nose. It's her thing.

Furniture crashes over as Blondie runs into stuff while she runs around like a lunatic. The guys shout and try to intervene, but the woman is too worked up to stop, and my duck just continues to squawk, flap, and snap, which only makes Blondie more panicked.

When Penn suddenly walks in through the front door, his hazel eyes widen in surprise at the sight before him. "What the hell?"

Somehow, even with her hair all over the place, Blondie is able to see the open door, and she shoves Penn out of the doorway and bolts outside, still screaming like a banshee.

My duck has a really good hold on her hair by now. She's just about to go in for the money shot and get Blondie's entire nose when someone plucks her off Blondie's head and holds her hostage in his hands. My duck swivels her neck to look behind her to see who intervened.

Penn.

Fur pops out on his hands where he's holding my duck, but he manages to suppress his shift. My duck desperately tries to get back at the bitch who dared touch her rutting shifter, but it's no use; Penn's hold is too tight.

Blondie stands in front of us, gasping in the front yard. Her hair is a tangled mess, and every time my duck snaps her beak in the woman's direction, she flinches and shrieks a little.

When Herrick and Lafe come outside and start walking over to Blondie to check on her, my duck squawks at them in warning. They stop in their tracks immediately. *Ha!* My duck stretches her neck smugly.

Blondie lifts a shaking hand to point at me. "Y-you have a pet duck?" she asks shrilly.

Lafe starts laughing, but it's quickly cut off when Herrick smacks him on the back of the head. "Yes," Herrick answers simply.

"Well, your stupid duck is fucking crazy!" she shrieks.

Her words make my duck freak out again, and images of crapping all over her blonde hair pops into our head. Yeah. Getting bird crap on our enemies' heads is just as fulfilling as it sounds. Oh, and now my duck has spotted her car, and she wants to crap all over that, too. I fully support the idea.

My duck tries to get out of Penn's hold to mete out some serious bird poop punishment, but he just taps her beak with his finger. "Stop that, you naughty thing," he reprimands her. "You've made your point. Herrick is very sorry. Aren't you, Herrick?" Penn asks, looking over at him.

Blondie gapes at them. "You're apologizing to your *duck?* That thing just attacked me!"

"She doesn't like visitors," Lafe says with a smirk. He looks like he's thoroughly enjoying himself. "You'll have to excuse her bad behavior. She's very territorial."

"Who even has a duck for a pet?" the woman asks indignantly.

"She's got a point," Penn mumbles.

My duck snaps at his finger. "Ouch!" he exclaims, shaking

his hand. "That's it. You need a time out," he tells me. "Herrick, say goodbye to your friend."

To my utter surprise and delight, Herrick mumbles, "Sorry, I gotta go. Nice meeting you."

Blondie shrieks. "Nice *meeting me?* You asshole!"

She wrenches off her heels and chucks them at his head one after the other. They land like four feet away from him, but at least she gave it the ol' college try. With one last huff, she storms to her car and peels out of the driveway. My duck holds her beak up high in victory.

When the woman is finally out of sight, Penn puts me down on the grass. All three guys surround me like hot towers of doom.

"Alright, Addie. Shift back," Penn orders.

My duck looks at him like he's an idiot. She ruffles her feathers and starts waddling around the lawn instead.

"Look at her ducking go," Lafe snickers.

"Aderyn Locke. You will shift back right *now,*" Penn says sternly, trying to order me around all alpha-like. My duck doesn't listen of course, but I think it's pretty hot.

Ignoring him completely, my duck struts right past them and through the open front door. She half-walks, half-flies to the kitchen. Before the guys can stop her, she raids the cupboards and knocks over a box of crackers. My duck goes to town on those bad boys.

Lafe watches with amusement as she buries her head in

the box and starts chowing down. "I guess she wanted a quacker," he jokes.

I can't even appreciate his attempt at lightening the mood. My duck is pissed that Herrick brought home another female, and to be honest, so am I. The very reason he's in a rut is because of *me*. The only one that should be reaping the benefits of his constant arousal for the immediate future is yours truly.

It's an unspoken shifter rule. You don't just go out and do the dirty with someone else when the female you rutted with is still riding her heatwave. And even more than that, you never, *ever* have sex with someone else when you've just answered a mate-call. I feel utterly betrayed. And my duck is feeling *very* territorial. And when she feels territorial...

One second, my duck is finishing off the last of the crackers and the next, she pops a squat, bears down and...

"Quack!"

Lafe's mouth drops open. "Did she just..."

Penn blinks. "Lay an egg on the counter? Yup."

Yeah...my duck kind of lays eggs when she's feeling territorial. It's her way of breaking in the nest, so to speak.

The guys just stare at it. Awkward.

My duck looks down at her impressively-sized egg and nods once in satisfaction. She gives her mates a look, quacking reproachfully like, *"Here assholes, I laid you an egg. Leave that there so bitches know you're taken,"* kind of thing.

Finished with her crackers and laying (literally) down the law, my duck flies down from the counter and waddles into the bathroom. Then she hops into the bathtub and waits politely.

"What is she doing now?" Lafe asks, as the guys file into the bathroom.

Penn smirks and then reaches over to turn on the water. My duck honks at him until he gets the temperature just right. Then she quacks contentedly and starts to paddle her legs in the water.

"So, she's just gonna..." Lafe motions his hand at me. "Wade around in the bath?" he asks, and I notice that he's holding the egg in his hand.

"She likes the water," Herrick mumbles.

As if the guys suddenly remember he's there, Penn and Lafe turn on him. "What the hell were you thinking bringing another female here?" Penn snaps.

Herrick stuffs his hands in his pockets and actually looks a bit guilty. "I wasn't thinking. I just needed to take the edge off, you know?" He darts a look at me before looking away again. "I didn't think Addie was coming back."

My duck quacks aggressively at him. Yes, that's also a thing. My duck's quacks can be downright menacing.

"That was a dick move, and you know it," Penn says. "Whether you like it or not, you're mated to her. We all are. Show some respect." Penn shakes his head at him and then looks back at Lafe. "What was Addie doing back here, anyway?"

"I sorta followed her to the motel," Lafe admits.

Penn sighs but doesn't look surprised. "You bribed her to come back?"

Lafe shakes his head. "No. She was running from someone. I saw her in the parking lot and I was her getaway. There was a guy in a SUV who tried to tail us, but I lost him after a couple of miles. I think she might've been attacked."

"She was *what?*" Penn barks, instantly furious. His body tenses, and even Herrick's face darkens with anger. "What do you mean you think she was attacked?"

"Well, I actually didn't get the details yet. I'd just gotten her inside and we were going to talk about it, but…" Lafe trails off, running his fingers over the egg in his palm.

…But we started feeling each other up and were about to get it on, and then Herrick brought home Blondie, so my duck lost her shit.

I guess Penn realizes what Lafe isn't saying, because he narrows his hazel eyes on him and clenches his fists. Geez Louise. Does he hate me so much that he doesn't even want Lafe to be around me? That's pretty shitty, to be honest. It's not like I purposely triggered the mate-call to trap them into being with me. It just happened and all of us went with it. The logical thing to do is to at least try to see if we can build a relationship.

If we just sever the bond, then our animals will be crushed. We might never be able to mate with anyone else for as long as we live, and shifters can live for hundreds of years. That would be a lonely existence. I've always dreamed about the day I'd find the shifter that my animal and I would want to send out the mate-call to. I always pictured it would be someone I'd been dating for awhile—someone who accepted my animal and me. Not a trio of predator outsiders who don't want me. It makes this whole thing even worse, considering the bonded shifters that I know in Pack Aberrant always seem so amazing together.

Mate bonds are special. The bond connects you in a magical way. Some shifters have such strong mate bonds, that they're able to communicate telepathically. It's rare, but it happens. Aside from that, it's supposed to be like finding your other half, and the sex is supposed to be off the charts. That last one at least, I can claim as true.

Now that my duck has eaten and she's happily wading around in the water, she loosens her hold on the control over our body. *Finally.* In a flash, I shift back into my human form and stretch out in the full-length bathtub with a groan.

All three guys look down at me, startled. Their eyes go from concerned about my possible attack, to heated as they take in my naked body. I bristle a little. They want me, but not my duck, and it just doesn't work that way.

I decide to ignore their lustful looks and chalk it up to my heatwave and their newly formed bonds. Speaking of heatwave, I think my temperature is rising again. Which means I might be entering into my second wave pretty soon.

"Could someone pass me the bubbles?" I ask.

Lafe and Penn both dive for the bottle, but Penn smirks when his hand closes around it first. Lafe grumbles, but turns on the water again while Penn pours in some soap. Bubbles quickly collect around me and I dunk my head under, flattening my hair back before coming up and sighing contentedly. At least they have a big jacuzzi tub. Silver linings and all that. "That's your cue to leave," I tell them, closing my eyes as I lean back.

"But the attack—" Penn begins to argue.

"I'll tell you *after* I've finished with my bath," I say with a pointed look. "Oh, and you can just put that egg in the fridge or toss it," I tell Lafe.

Lafe holds the egg against his chest protectively. "What? No. Isn't it…you know…our chick?"

I raise a brow, doing my best not to laugh. "Duckling. And no. It's not fertilized. I'm on shifter birth control."

"Oh. Well, it's a nice egg," he says, studying it.

"Thank you," I say proudly, my duck smug as shit. It *is* a nice egg. "But I'm still pissed at you guys," I add, glaring at Herrick in particular, then I cock my head at Lafe. "Well, except for you."

Lafe beams arrogantly and then struts out of the bathroom with the egg in hand like he's king shit, while the other two follow tensely behind him.

When the door is closed and I'm alone, I soap up my hair and body and then relax in the hot water, wishing I could wash away this entire day. My walk of shame, the motel attack, the Blondie incident—I'm at my limit. Luckily, water has always been able to calm me.

When I'm done washing and soaking, I have a much clearer head, and my duck is happy to relax in the background again. After I dry off, I find that someone left a clean pair of sweatpants and another t-shirt for me, so I quickly pull them on. The pants are way too big, so I have to roll up the ankles and pull the drawstring super tight, but it'll work until I can get Zoey to bring me some clothes.

I find a comb—probably Lafe's since his hair is the longest —and run it through my wet and tangled locks. When that's done, I look in the mirror, and...I still look a bit homeless, to be honest. Except now I look like a homeless person who was stuck in a rainstorm. Oh well.

I leave the bathroom and walk into the living room, finding all of the guys are there waiting for me. Lafe is lounging on the recliner, Penn is poised against the arm of the couch, and Herrick has his arms crossed over by the window that he's looking out.

"Okay," I say, walking in. "Do you want the short version or the long version?"

"Just tell us," Penn says, his body full of tension as he watches me.

"Short version it is," I say with a nod as I lean against the far wall. "The guy I went out with last night? Yeah, turns out I was a job instead of a date."

"What kind of job?" Penn questions.

I can tell that he's the pseudo leader between the three of them. Herrick might be a tad bigger and scarier, but Penn screams authority in the way he takes the lead in every situation.

"The kind of job where he was hired by a rival pack to get close to the person who messed up their bank robbery. AKA, yours truly."

Penn's blond brows furrow. "That human was hired to trick you into a date?"

I nod. "Yep, to get close to me apparently, and then lure me somewhere. I don't even want to think about what would've happened if I'd gotten into his car last night when my first wave hit." I cross my arms protectively in front of me, and all three of the guys tense. "I guess it's a good thing you three came along when you did and I ditched him. Otherwise, I'd probably be in some underground cell at Pack Rockhead right now, and who knows what they would've done while I was in heat."

The implication of my words hang heavily in the air.

He does it so quickly that I don't even see him move, but the next thing I know, Lafe has picked up the side table lamp and hurled it against the wall. I squeal and cover my ears as it shatters, but he's already in front of me, his hands gripping my arms. "Sorry," he says quickly. "I just...I fucking can't...Just the thought of you being hurt..." His whole body is shaking with fury that wants to let loose.

Penn comes up behind him. "Let go of Addie before *you* hurt her," he says sternly.

Lafe blinks and looks down at where he's holding me by the arms. He quickly drops his hold, leaving red marks behind from how hard he was clutching me. "Shit! I'm sorry. I didn't mean—"

"Hey," I say, touching his arm. "It's okay." He blows out a breath, but I can tell that he's upset that he might've hurt me. He didn't, but my skin is sensitive, so I'm easily marked up.

Lafe's volatile reaction surprised me, because he seems like the calmest and happiest of the trio, but then again, with our new bond, his mate instincts will be riding him hard, which includes extreme protectiveness and possessiveness. Also, out of the three, he seems to like me the most, so no wonder he freaked out when he realized what might have happened. Even Penn and Herrick are visibly upset, with grinding teeth and clenched jaws.

I have to be careful not to mistake their shifter mating instinct for anything else though. It's not as if Herrick actually likes me, despite the way he's cracking his knuckles like he wants to conjure Mario in front of him and punch him in the face.

Lafe starts pacing around the room and Penn eyes him warily for a moment, making sure he isn't going to hurl anything else against the wall.

"Are you trying to say that Pack Rockhead organized that robbery and that they attacked you today at the motel?" Herrick asks.

"That's exactly what I'm saying."

He shakes his head. "Why would they do that? They're a prominent and strong pack. They don't need to use humans for robberies."

"Why would Pack Rockhead have been involved?" Penn asks.

I look at them like they're idiots. "Why does *anyone* rob a freaking bank? For money, obviously."

"But their pack is centuries old. I highly doubt they have money problems," Herrick replies.

I can't believe what I'm hearing. "Are you seriously defending them right now?"

Herrick scoffs. "Don't get dramatic. All I'm saying is, are you sure it was them?"

I balk at him. "You are unbelievable! You stand there, after being in town for what, a couple of weeks, and act like you know better than I do?" I snap. "You don't know shit, Herrick."

"Alright, alright," Penn interferes. "Calm down, Addie."

"No," I say with a swipe of my hand through the air. "He's calling me a liar, and I won't stand for it."

Penn sighs. "That's not what he's saying. He's saying—"

"I *know* what he's saying," I say, cutting him off. "He's

saying that he'll always take another preds' side over someone like me. He'd rather give the benefit of the doubt to *them,* a pack he doesn't even know, than give it to *me,* the female he's mated to. All because I'm a duck from Pack Aberrant—a shifter not nearly good enough for him and his hotshot coyote, isn't that right, Herrick?" I challenge, practically spitting my words.

Herrick says nothing, just clenches his jaw and glares at me with his dark eyes and brooding expression.

"I didn't get the impression that they were the kind of shifters to hire humans for illegal activities," Penn says carefully.

I bristle at that and focus on him instead. "So you've met them? You've met Pack Rockhead?"

Penn's eyes shift to Herrick nervously. "We, uh…we applied to join them."

A bitter laugh barks out of me and I rub a hand down my face. "Of course you did."

"Addie…" Lafe begins.

I shake my head and hold my hands out to ward them off. "No. I'm done. You were right to want to sever the bond. I refuse to be mated to you three. You stay away from me, and I'll stay away from you. Your rut will be over in a few days so long as we stay separated. Go fuck whoever you want," I tell Herrick crudely.

My whole heart hurts. My animal is practically weeping. "Our bond will eventually break after no contact," I choke out the words, pissed when I realize a tear has escaped and is running down my cheek. "Have fun joining Pack Asshole. You'll fit right in."

I turn on my heel and stalk out the front door, slamming it behind me. This time, none of them follow me out, and I'm relieved, because as soon as my feet hit the grass, more hot tears start falling down my face. Miserable and aching from the distance of my mates, I perch on the curb with my head in my hands. I can hear the guys yelling at each other from inside, but I tune them out.

My emotions are going haywire, and the strained mating bond isn't helping things. It's like everything inside of me is at war. On the one hand, I'm pissed that the guys met with Rockhead to possibly join that pack, and I'm hurt that they doubt who attacked me and why. But I also want to go back in there and curl up against Lafe and let him finish what we started earlier, because I can tell I'm about to hit my second wave.

Luckily, I don't have to wait long for Zoey to show up, since I texted her from Lafe's phone earlier. I hop off the curb as soon as she pulls up, and practically launch myself into her car. Unlike hobo me, Zoey looks cute in a white romper with skulls and roses all over it. She takes one look at my disheveled appearance and tear-stained cheeks and her expression turns worried.

"Oh, honey. What happened? Was it Mario? I knew I shouldn't have let you leave with him. I could just kick myself right now," she curses.

I grab her purse that's stuffed on the floorboard at my feet and root around for the package of tissues I know are there. Her purse is like a pit of buried treasure. You need it? She probably has it. Tampons, mints, sweet snacks, salty snacks, spicy snacks—because she argues that you have to have all three options—a wine opener, money in three different currencies, and is that...yep, that's a dagger.

After shoving aside a paperback and a sample pod of laundry detergent, I finally find the packet I'm looking for. I pluck a tissue out and blow my nose before wiping my eyes.

"Not Mario," I tell her. "It's a long story, but I ended up going home with three coyote shifters and I accidentally mated myself to all three of them. It didn't go well once they found out what my animal was, so I left, but then I was sort of attacked by Pack Rockhead."

Her eyes widen in surprise. "Oh, shit."

"Yeah."

I turn to look out the window when I hear the front door slam shut, and see Penn stalking toward us. My stomach flips uncomfortably. I can't deal with him anymore.

Zoey hisses. "You want me to bite him? I have a lot of venom stored up right now," Zoey offers seriously. "I don't even have to fully shift. Just a partial and I can bring these babies out," she says, pointing to her canines.

"That's okay," I say, sniffing.

"You sure? If I got him really good, I could even cause internal hemorrhaging," she says proudly.

"You're such a good friend," I tell her. "Let's go. I don't want to talk to him."

"You got it."

She puts the car into drive and takes off, flipping Penn off as she goes. I watch him in the side mirror as he stops and watches us go with a glower on his face.

One second, he's standing in the middle of the road, scowling at me, and the next, he's shifted into his coyote and is racing toward the trees. It's the first time I've seen his animal, and seeing it makes my stomach flip again, but for a totally different reason. He's impressive, with the perfect amount of strength and speed. I wrench my eyes away, and lean back in the seat, and Zoey reaches over to squeeze my hand in silent comfort.

She races down the street, and neither of us say another word, because we don't have to. This is what it's like in the life of a misfit. We'll always be the ones waiting at the curb like yesterday's trash.

ADDIE

"Do I need to stage an intervention?"

I crack open one eye and see Zoey and Aspen standing over me, both of them wearing frowns and rubber rain boots. I open my other eye and look up, but there isn't a cloud to be seen in the morning sky.

Wearily, I run a wet hand over my face and try to get my bearings. I see that I'm in the backyard of our warehouse, soaking in the pool I slept in all night. I was finally able to pass out after my fourth bottle of wine. All of the bottles are bobbing in the water next to me.

When colors catch my eye, I look over at the back ware-house wall where a new addition has appeared. Zoey and Aspen follow my gaze, and the three of us stare at the new graffiti that's now decorating the metal wall.

"Looks like our resident tagger struck again," Zoey says as she studies the pair of intricate wings painted on the building.

"It's pretty," Aspen comments.

I squint my eyes. "Is that...does that say *don't fuck with our duck?*" I say with a croaky voice.

Zoey and Aspen both tilt their heads to the left so they can better read the scrawled font. "Huh. Guess our tagger doesn't like that your three mates are being total assholes."

Someone in our pack secretly graffitis our buildings. There are ongoing bets on which one of the misfits it is. My money is on the tortoise.

Settling back, I rub my aching temples. It's harder for shifters to get drunk, but four bottles of homemade wine will do it. I look down at the pool and frown. "You took my hose."

Aspen tightens her hold on the garden hose like she's worried I'll try to snag it from her. I like to have my water move, so I'd left the water dripping all night. It took me a good five minutes to get the perfect trickle from the spigot. With just a bit of flow, it made the water lap against my skin just like it would in a lake, and it settled me enough to get some sleep.

"It took a lot of finagling to get the water pressure just right," I tell her with irritation.

Ignoring my tone, she turns the hose off and then tosses it onto the ground. A small splash comes up from the impact. "You flooded the backyard," she points out.

I lean over the edge of the polka-dotted shallow pool to get a look. And yep, my trickling hose did, in fact, flood the backyard. The grassy area all around has a couple inches of water. The rain boots that they're wearing make more sense now.

"Whoopsie daisy," I offer.

They exchange a look before Zoey crosses her arms and looks down at me again. "Addie, please tell me you did not sleep in this kiddie pool all night long."

Indignant at her tone, I try to sit up a bit, but the bright blue plastic of the inflatable kiddie pool is slippery as hell, so I glide right back down, making the water splash in my face and the plastic squeak embarrassingly loud. The pool is only about four feet in diameter, so my legs hang awkwardly over the edge, my fingers and toes are like prunes, and I have water lodged in one of my ears. Maybe sleeping in a kiddie pool was not my best idea.

Instead of trying to sit up again, I settle for leaning my head back on the blow-up donut that I used as a pillow last night, and try to do that thing where I tilt my chin up so I can look haughty. Instead, I tilt it too much, sending the donut flying back, and my head falls into the water with a splash. I come up sputtering and spitting, choking a little on the water that went down the wrong tube.

Zoey shakes her head at me. "This is low. Even for you."

"Can one of you at least help me up?" I ask, feeling crankier by the second now that water went up my nose. It's not a nice feeling.

"You made your kiddie pool bed. Now you have to paddle in it," she quips.

Stinger, one of the enforcers for the pack, comes strolling out with a plate of cocktail shrimp that he's tossing into his mouth and swallowing whole. When he sees me in my duck-ini (bikini with ducks on it), sopping wet in the kiddie pool and glaring at the girls, he grins at the sight.

"Talk about wet dreams," he quips.

I point at him. "I will let my duck bite your nose off while you sleep."

He wags his eyebrows. "Kinky."

He sidles up between Zoey and Aspen, settling his elbow on Aspen's shoulder before offering her a shrimp. She wrinkles her nose and politely declines. He's wearing green flip flops, bright orange board shorts, and a gray, fancy collared polo that in no way goes with the bottom half of his outfit. When he's not in uniform for guard duty at the gate, he dresses like someone confused about whether he's on spring break or going golfing.

"Do I want to know why you look like you slept in the kiddie pool all night?" he asks conversationally as he eats another shrimp. He's not even dipping it in anything. Just eating the cold things as-is.

"I like the water," I grumble.

Stinger chomps on another bite. "Can't fault you there."

When he notices the graffiti, he stops eating for five seconds to take it in. "Does that say, *don't fuck our duck?*"

"No!" I say with irritation.

He opens his mouth, no doubt to tease me mercilessly, but his phone rings, interrupting him. He pulls it out from his pocket and with a wink at Aspen, he saunters back inside to answer it.

Zoey sighs and kneels down. "Come on. Let's get you out of there."

"I can do it myself," I say stubbornly.

I try to get out of the pool again, and this time, I actually manage to pull my leg back and get a knee under me as I turn. But...yeah, it's slippery. I cause more of the terribly embarrassing plastic squeaking noises and I scramble for purchase, while trying not to completely eat shit (again). My arms and legs flail around as I try to haul myself out. It really shouldn't be this difficult, but it's like someone poured baby oil all over the thing. Plastic should not be this slippery. I half-climb, half-fall over the side of it, until I land face-first onto the flooded grass.

Head planted into the muddy lawn, feet still kicking in the kiddie pool, and ass up on the inflatable side. That's how my poor alpha father-figure finds me.

Spitting out mud from my mouth, I hear shoes squelching on the flooded lawn before Hugo's boots appear in front of my face. "Hellhound's balls, kid. What are you doing?"

I look up and give him a wave from this terrible position. "Hey, Alpha."

I hear him sigh, and then he hooks his hands under my armpits and hauls me up. Once I'm on my feet again, I swipe the mud away from my face and try to give him an innocent smile. He cocks a bushy brow at me before turning his head to look at the others. "Do I even want to know?"

"She's having a bit of a personal break down while in the process of severing *all three* of her mate bonds," Zoey says, waving a hand at me. I glare at her, but she just shrugs, not sorry at all about spilling my secret. She tosses me a towel, and some clothes, so I quickly dry off before tugging on the oversized t-shirt and shorts.

Hugo's eyes come back to me. "Severing? I thought you were discussing it."

Okay, so I sort of led him to believe we were discussing it. And by sort of, I mean that I *told* him we were discussing it.

"I didn't want you to worry," I tell him.

"Kid, what did I tell you before? You're my pack. I always worry about my pack," he reprimands me. "Now, how bad is it?"

I hate the fact that my eyes start burning right then. I'm not a crier. I'm not one of those chicks who cries at commercials or sappy movies. But this week has been complete hell, and my emotions are going crazy, and every second that I'm awake, I feel like I'm being ripped into pieces. Trying to let the bond sever is painful physically, but the other side effects are just as distressing. Like how my animal won't come out because she's depressed, and how I keep feeling this tug in my gut, like my body is trying to get me to go to them.

"She isn't eating, Alpha. She's barely sleeping. All she does is sit around in the water, wherever she can find it," Zoey tells him.

"She took a four hour shower yesterday," Aspen pipes in, her singsong voice making it sound not so bad. "I finally had to pick the lock on the bathroom door. The shower was ice cold and her teeth were chattering when I dragged her out." Okay, so that sounds a little bad, even with her princess-y voice.

"The water makes me feel better," I mumble, feeling more and more embarrassed by the second.

Not only do all of my packmates know that I accidentally mated with three shifters, but they also know that those mates don't want me, which is why I'm suffering with the separation pain. It was magnified since I was still in heat too, but luckily, that's over. Severing a mate bond is a painful process, and can take weeks for it to snap. Which means I might have to suffer with this awful sensation in my chest for another month.

Hugo's face softens as he takes me in. "What about your new job?"

"She starts tomorrow," Zoey answers for me.

"And those three pricks? You heard from them?" Miserable, I shake my head no, and Hugo grunts with obvious disapproval. "Those little shits. I'm gonna wring their necks."

"Please don't," I say. "I don't want anyone to feel obligated to be my mate. That would be the worst." I rub at the spot on my neck where the guys bit me. It's hot to the touch, like they permanently altered my skin there, even though they didn't leave a mark. "I'll get through this, and then the bonds will sever and it'll be over," I say, trying to sound more confident than I am.

Hugo shakes his head, a deep crease between his brows. "I don't like this. I've never heard of a shifter breaking multiple mate bonds at the same time. It's hard enough to do it with just one connection. This could be dangerous, Addie. It could potentially kill you."

I swallowed hard, my eyes widening. "Really?"

I didn't want to freaking die! I just didn't want three mates who didn't want me for duck's sake.

"Really. Which is why I'm ordering you, as your alpha, to go talk to them. I won't let you get hurt, kid. So take care of it, or I'll drag those sons of bitches back here by their tails. Got it?"

I didn't know how I could possibly promise him that. Sure, I didn't want the bond to kill me, but I might actually die of pride, because the very last thing I wanted to do was crawl back to them and beg them to stay with me. I'd rather be banned from the lake.

Hugo must see the conflict on my face, because he opens his mouth to argue with me, except we're interrupted suddenly when Stinger comes back outside. "Alpha!"

Hugo turns to face his enforcer, and Stinger walks up to

him. He must've been in the process of changing into his guard uniform, because he has his black cargo pants on now, but his polo shirt is still the same as before, and he only managed to get one black boot on before rushing out here.

"What is it?"

"There's trouble at the front gate."

Hugo nods, his expression turned hard and protective. "Alright, let's go check it out."

Stinger hops on one foot to get his other boot on while following Hugo. He strips his polo next, revealing an impressive chest, and yanks on his black enforcer shirt. When he catches Aspen watching, he grins and sends her a wink. She turns bright red and hurries inside the house.

"Stinger, you'll ride with me," Hugo says, as he walks around the back of the house to get to his Jeep. I start heading inside with Zoey and Aspen, but Hugo stops me. "Come on, kid. You're sticking with me until I can get you and your mates together."

"Alpha…"

"No arguments. Let's go."

Hugo gets behind the wheel of his Jeep, and I climb in the backseat while Stinger takes the front. He has his phone to his ear, hearing reports from one of the other enforcers. Hugo takes off, his big tires making a rut in the road as he guns it back to the gate. I hold on to the back of Stinger's seat, worry clenching my stomach.

What if it's Pack Rockhead come to cause trouble? They're a strong, pred-only pack, and we're primarily prey animals. Sure, we have good defenses, but nothing is one-hundred-percent safe.

If Pack Rockhead decides that they want our land or to take out our shifters, this could go very badly. Hugo is strong, and he's made sure our enforcers are too, but they can't fight an entire pack on their own, and most of us in Pack Aberrant aren't physically strong animals when it comes to fighting.

But there's also this other little voice in my head that keeps rearing up, no matter how much I try to dash it away. *What if it's the guys?*

I don't want to get my hopes up, but I can't help it. What if they finally came here to talk to me? What if they feel the intensity of this mate bond as much as I do? My stomach twists and turns, and all I can do is try to stop the barrage of what-ifs that are crashing through my brain. My mate bond pulses with longing.

Stinger keeps listening to the other end and relaying back information to Hugo, but they're talking in enforcer-code language that I just don't understand. Hugo cuts the wheel sharply around the corner and then flies the car past the rest of the housing. We make it to the front gate in record time, and he's already parked the Jeep and hopped out with Stinger before the dust from the tires has settled.

"Stay in the car, kid," he tells me before slamming the door shut.

I scramble to the driver's seat and roll down the window, my eyes scanning the fence. It's solid, thick iron, with spikes at the top and barbs beneath. The gate is closed, but there are five enforcers in a line, and another three in the tower, all of them male, and they're clearly speaking to someone on the other side.

I can't hear what they're saying, but I see Igor, Hugo's second in command, step forward and quickly fill Hugo in on the details as he strides up. Igor is a huge dude with a bald head, massive biceps, and a neck thicker than my thigh. He doesn't say much, but one look from him can get pretty much everyone to fall in line to do Hugo's bidding.

After talking for a moment, Hugo makes a hand signal to open the gate, and I practically hang out of the window to see who's on the other side. Hugo left the keys in the ignition, so if shit goes bad and Pack Rockhead is on the other side waiting to attack us, I'll plough right into them and take out as many of them as I can.

Heartless? Maybe. But I grew up with them, and I know their pack motto. "Step on the small and claim it all." It wasn't exactly a comfortable bedtime nursery rhyme. If they get it in their heads that they want to take us out, they won't hesitate to do just that, using any sneaky, dishonorable tactics they can. I won't go down without a fight. This time, I won't run from them.

I have one hand on the keys and one hand on the outside of the window, my body poised up, straining to see past the enforcers as the gate slowly slides open. But what I see on the other side makes me falter. It's not Pack Rockhead.

Officer MacQuilley is standing on the other side, his cop car parked at the gate. He has a shiner around his eye and I can tell by the scowl on his face that he's ready for this morning to be over, even though it's barely past eight. I'm confused about why there's a big hubbub over Mac. He's an ally for us, and comes over sometimes to relay information to Hugo.

Mac is human, but his grandmother was a shifter, so he carries some shifter DNA, and he knows about our kind. It's good to have him as our eyes and ears, and unlike some of the dirty cops in town, he doesn't run information through Pack Rockhead. Mac is a solid guy and he helps us out when he can.

In return, we make sure to help keep an eye on Pack Rockhead and pass along information that Mac should know. Seeing as there's no immediate danger, I slip out of the Jeep and make my way over. Hearing the door shut, Stinger turns and shakes his head at me, but returns his focus on Hugo.

"Mac," Hugo says, striding forward. "What do you got?"

"Sorry to run over here like this without calling ahead," Mac says, running a hand through his orange hair. "But time was an issue. But if I hadn't crossed into Aberrant pack land, they would've gone over my head and taken her to Rockhead."

Hugo frowns. "Who?"

Mac points back to his cop car, and all of our focus goes there. "Got the burglary call in around seven AM this morning. She was found inside the hardware store."

"A shifter?" Hugo asked.

Mac nods. "She's gotta be."

I can't help the crushing disappointment that sinks into me. It's not the guys. They haven't come for me.

"She shifted in front of you?" Hugo asks.

Dread coils in my stomach. If the shifter in his cop car really did openly shift in front of a human, then our own shifter government would punish her according to shifter law. Sometimes that meant immeasurable fines, but it would definitely mean imprisonment, and no shifter wanted that.

It was common knowledge that they used warlock magic in Cane prisons, and the magic there makes shifters unable to change into their animals. And if our animals are kept suppressed like that for years at a time...it can lead to madness or death.

So it's a relief when Mac shakes his head. "No. I knew she was a shifter because she's been collared."

I hear Stinger curse under his breath and several of the other enforcers shift uneasily. I can feel fury rolling in waves off of Hugo, as his alpha energy slips out from his rage. To collar a shifter is a barbaric act, but our shifter governments have been unable to overturn the ancient law that allows it.

To this day, vampires, warlocks—hell, even other shifters —are legally allowed to collar a shifter and bring them into servitude if a contract is agreed upon. Centuries ago, it used to be done to feral shifters who had committed grave crimes, as a way for them to atone without being put to death. But the punishment had been twisted and used in other more nefarious ways. It wasn't something commonly done anymore, since there'd been an outcry against the form of slavery, but the law had never changed.

"She's lucky I was the one to take the call. That prick Holder was on his way as my back up. I knew that if he got a look at her, he'd know that the metal around her neck weren't no necklace, and he'd scurry her off to the dicks at Rockhead. Didn't want that to happen, especially with her being female and all, so I hightailed it outta there. She didn't make it easy, though," Mac added, gesturing to his bruised and swollen eye. "She's got a mean right hook."

"I can't keep a rogue shifter here against her will."

"I understand, but I figured you could talk to her," Mac says. "I couldn't just let her go. Half of the town is Pack Rockhead territory. Maybe you can talk some sense into her, because she won't listen to me."

Hugo looks to Stinger and one of the other enforcers, Joseph and nods to them. Wordlessly, the two males stride forward to the cop car to let the female out.

As soon as the door is opened though, she sends a fierce kick to Stinger's shin, making him stumble back, and then nails him in the chin with a hammer hit using the heel of her palm.

Stinger barely manages to stay on his feet when she hurls a fist into his stomach, and then she pushes past his keeled over form to sprint for the woods, but Joseph overtakes her by wrapping his arms around her middle and hauling her back, kicking and cursing.

"Let go of me!"

It takes another two enforcers to help Joseph bring her inside the gate and stop her from hurting anyone. Stinger limps over, a terrific scowl over his usually easygoing face.

She keeps fighting, straining to kick, bite, or punch anyone she can reach. She's striking looking, with the left half of her hair solid black, and the right side so blonde that it looks white. The half-hair color carries from her ponytail, down to her long, blunt bangs, giving off a Cruella vibe, except cooler. She has pale, milky skin, which is only highlighted by the torn fishnet tights she's wearing under ripped shorts, combat boots, and a worn leather jacket.

"Enough!" Hugo roars, making everyone in the vicinity shudder with the alpha powers that roll off of him.

The female immediately freezes, only because an alpha's magic, especially one as strong as Hugo, is too powerful to ignore.

"If you continue to harm members of my pack, I will set you loose, and you will be picked up by Pack Rockhead in a matter of hours. Believe me, you don't want that. We're trying to help you," Hugo tells her.

She pants, sneering at him, and I can see everyone is

honing in on the thick iron collar wrapped around her neck. Except for me. Because as soon as I see her face, I recognize her.

"Holy moley."

I rush forward, pushing past enforcers on my way. "Jetta?" Her head snaps over at my voice, and her dark eyes lock with mine. "It's me. Aderyn Locke."

Her dark, thick brows bend together in a frown as she takes me in, but then recognition dawns on her. "Addie?"

Hugo looks at me with a questioning scowl. "Tell your friend to calm down, kid," he says.

"You're safe here," I tell Jetta. "I swear it."

She snorts disbelievingly. "I'm not safe anywhere."

I haven't seen her since I was fourteen years old. We'd been kids back then, but I'd know her anywhere—even with her extreme dye job. She was the only shifter to have ever been my friend, even if it hadn't lasted long.

When I knew her, she'd had plain glossy black hair, but she'd worn the same fierce expression on her face that she's wearing now, her striking eyes narrowed suspiciously over her prominent cheekbones.

"Please, Jetta. Let us try to help you."

She hesitates, wary of me, but after another sweep of her eyes, she finally relents with a terse nod. "Fine."

With a look from Hugo, the other two enforcers let go of

her and move away, but Joseph moves to the side, keeping hold of her left arm just in case.

"How do you know each other?" Hugo asks.

I share a look with Jetta, and I can see that the fire behind her eyes is still there, just like it was before. And just like I remember that fire, I remember how private and prideful she always was. She would detest having me talk openly about her in front of everyone like this.

"Can we talk in private?" I ask Hugo.

He purses his lips and watches me for a moment before turning back to Jetta. He takes a menacing step forward, and when she tries to back up, Joseph holds her in place. "You are here on my pack land as a guest. Which means you are beholden to my word and law. You will not cause harm to my pack. Is that understood?"

She grinds her jaw in stubborn anger, but bites out, "Understood."

Hugo looks over to Mac. "Thanks, Mac."

Mac nods and walks back to his car. "I wrote it up in the report that she fled. Don't know if Rockhead already caught her scent. If they did, it could bring them back here to you," he says with caution.

"I'll deal with Rockhead. Thanks for your help."

Mac raises a hand in a wave before getting in his car and pulling away.

"Igor, you stay here. I want your eyes peeled in case Rock-head comes sniffing around. And have the enforcers do a perimeter mark. We can try to cover up her scent at our gate, at least."

Igor nods and looks around at the enforcers. "Everyone back to their posts," he says, starting to issue out orders.

"Stinger and Joseph, you escort her," Hugo says. "Addie, with me. We'll talk in my office."

ADDIE

I'm sitting with Jetta inside Hugo's office alone. Shortly after we got to the building not far from the front gate, he took a phone call. Joseph and Stinger stayed outside the door keeping watch.

"You still fidget when you're nervous, I see."

My eyes snap up to Jetta. We're sitting in matching leather chairs, except she's lounging back in hers, looking as cool as cucumber, whereas my back is ramrod straight and I keep picking at a tear in the leather armrest. I force myself to stop as I smile sheepishly. "Yeah. I guess I do."

"I remember you biting your nails down to the nubs."

I pull back my fingers to look at my short nails. "Still do that, too," I laugh.

"You left your old pack."

She says it like a statement, but I can hear the questions behind it.

I nod. "Alpha Rourn issued me my fight or flight orders on the morning of my fifteenth birthday."

Jetta curses and shakes her head. "I hated that guy."

I hum in agreement. "We had that in common."

"So you ended up here?"

"Yep," I nod. "Hugo took me in. He's a good alpha," I tell her. "Nothing like Rourn or the others."

"What pack is this?"

"Aberrant."

This catches her by surprise, and her arched brows rise up. "Aberrant? As in the *Pack of Misfits?*"

I laugh at the nickname we've been given. "Yep, that's the one."

"And…" She leans in and sniffs me. "You're mated?"

I grimace slightly. "Kind of. It's...complicated."

I can see the wheels turning behind her eyes. But before she can voice any more questions, the door opens and Hugo comes striding inside. He closes the door after him and moves to sit behind his large wooden desk. Behind him is a shelf filled with all sorts of hand-carved wooden figurines of a mishmash of different animals.

"Okay. I'm listening," he says, sitting down.

When Jetta says nothing, I clear my throat. "I met Jetta when I was fourteen. She was living with a band of travelling rogues."

"Family?" he asks her.

Jetta shakes her head. "Hell no. Those assholes took me from a human orphanage when I was one. Someone sniffed me out I guess. Perfect for them, because they preferred to grow their numbers with unattached shifters that they could mold and use."

"Use for what?" Hugo asks.

"Fighting for Troupe Delirium."

My stomach roiled, remembering the first time her rogue troupe had visited Rockhead. Their small group travelled to different packs all over the country and to other magical groups too, as a means of entertainment.

Watching rogues fight each other, sometimes in human form and sometimes in their animal form, was as barbaric as it sounded. But her troupe master had a flair for the dramatic. His shows always had an edge of theatrics. He didn't just train them to mindlessly fight, he trained them to be dancers, acrobats, magicians—anything to set his troupe above the rest. He even made his fighters take potions before they went out. Sometimes the potions would be hallucinogenic, sometimes they'd just make it impossible for them to shift. Whatever it was, it always made for a more interesting show.

Her troupe master was smart, too—he only took in rogues who had nowhere else to go, and then promised them riches if they just signed a contract and agreed to fight for a certain number of years. But those contracts basically made them indentured servants, unable to leave. Most of the rogues fought for years and then eventually died, still tied to that contract.

Suddenly, the collar makes sense to Hugo, and his frown deepens. "How long?"

She shrugs. "I'm twenty-five now."

I wince at the fact that this is all she's known. For twenty-four years, she's been forced to fight like a puppet put on display, while her troupe leader pulled all the strings.

"So you ran away?" Hugo surmises. "I thought the collars had trackers on them."

"They do. But my tracker broke in my last fight. I'm not even sure how, but I left as soon soon as I figured it out," she explains. "Funny thing about collars, though. It freaks humans out, but in our world?" She huffs out a frustrated breath. "Forget it. The Canes take one look at me with this, and they look the other way, like they're worried collars are contagious," she says with disgust.

"Unfortunately, it's still legal. And if you're under contract, then there's not a whole lot we can do," Hugo points out.

"I didn't ask to be brought here," Jetta says, bristling. "Open the gate and I'll leave right now."

"Relax," Hugo says with a wave of his hand. "I'm not going to put you out with Rockhead hot on your scent. You can stay here for a few days until they get off your trail, and then you're free to go," he tells her, and Jetta visibly relaxes. "Where's your troupe?"

"I left them in Arizona."

"But your troupe master will be looking for you," Hugo says, more as a statement than a question.

Jetta nods sharply and her fingers curl around the armrests of the chair, making my eyes focus on the sleeves of tattoos she has on both arms. She catches me looking and releases her grip, forcing her muscles to relax. "You have a lot more now," I say, nodding my head at them.

She'd had just a couple of tattoos when I first met her at Rockhead. It was right after Drag and Jordy had humiliated me in the cafeteria. I'd heard about Troupe Delirium coming, but I wasn't allowed to attend pack functions. As far as Alpha Rourn was concerned, I was his pack's dirty little secret. He never let me leave the Rockhead compound. He as too embarrassed by me—by having a non-pred living with his pack.

So the night that Delirium was set to be there, I'd snuck out of my room. Everyone was already gone to the training yard—the only space large enough for the troupe to perform. I'd gotten used to slinking around in the shadows, always forced to sneak around my own pack, so it was nothing new.

I could hear the cheers from a mile away. By the time I got to the training yard, it was full dark and the moon was full overhead. Rockhead was gathered in the viewing area, which was basically an open-air arena with wide steps that rose up in a semi-circle so we could view the yard below.

The entire space was packed full, and I had to watch from

the sidelines, where the arena backed up to the woods. I stayed crouched behind a boulder to watch, but when I finally saw what all the hype was about, my stomach roiled.

The shifters moved like dancers. There were five of them, and they switched off fighting one another, their movements fluid and almost graceful. This wasn't just gritty, plain fighting. This was a higher form of entertainment, made obvious by the stage props and costumes and choreography.

Jetta was dressed like the ground. She wore loincloths stained with mud and glued with rocks and grass, while the shifters surrounding her wore armor marked with bright yellow scorpions, looking like royal guards against a lowly miscreant. It was almost like watching a play, but aside from the costumes and rehearsed movements that led up to the the inevitable clash, the fight itself was one-hundred-percent real.

Jetta had fought valiantly, but she'd been a fifteen-year-old girl against five full grown, hardened men. She hadn't really stood a chance.

When the guards took her down, the Rockhead crowd clapped and cheered for more blood. Of course, the troupe master was all too glad to give them that. Jetta peeled herself off the stage, and from my vantage point, I watched her go, limping behind the temporary wall partition where the other troupe members were changing costumes or waiting to go on.

When the next round of fights started, this time in animal

form, I slunk back, keeping my eyes on Jetta. She was around my age, but that wasn't what fascinated me. It was how strong she was. I envied her. She fought against five male shifters and still walked away on her own two feet. But when I'd snuck into the performer's area and I saw her strip off her costume to tug on loose sweatpants and a shirt, that was when I'd first noticed the collar. It was also when she first noticed me.

It was weird. We didn't know each other. We'd never even seen one another before. And yet, we hit it off immediately. Maybe it was just because we were around the same age, but I think it had more to do with the fact that we hated being stuck living under the thumbs of ones who didn't care for us.

We'd snuck into the cafeteria and ate leftover pie and milk while we talked for hours. She was the first shifter I ever met who didn't look at me with hate, and I was the first to see the person behind the collar.

Her troupe had performed two more nights after that, and then they left, and I never saw her again. But I always remembered her. It seems almost surreal that she's here now, and our paths have crossed again.

"Master Kaazu likes his troupe to have a certain look," she says, glancing down at her arms.

Hugo looks to me. "Can you get her situated in the warehouse?"

"Of course," I nod.

"Good," he says, turning back to Jetta and running his

gaze over her collar. "We could try to get that off of you," he offers.

Jetta's hand goes up to the offending metal automatically. At least it's loose, so there's plenty of space around it that it can move freely, but it looks heavy, and the symbolism alone is enough to make me sick.

"I've been trying to get this thing off since I was eight. There's never been a shifter in the troupe that got theirs off."

"We'll try anyway," Hugo says.

For a split second, Jetta relaxes just the tiniest bit, and I see a fragment of hope in her eyes. "It's against Cane law to remove a shifter's collar unless it's with the explicit permission from that shifter's owner," she says, almost in challenge.

Hugo lifts a shoulder. "I don't care much for that law."

The corner of her lips tilt the tiniest bit, hinting at a smile. It's gone the next second, but I saw it, and I know Hugo did too. "Me either," she replies.

Hugo nods and then calls to Stinger and Joseph, and the enforcers quickly step inside. "Escort Jetta to the singles' warehouse. The same one as Addie. Get her set up in a room. Addie will be along shortly to show her around and get her what she needs, but I need a minute first."

The guys nod, and Jetta gets to her feet. She narrows her eyes at Joseph and Stinger and strides past them toward the door.

Just before she walks through it, she looks over her shoulder at Hugo and takes a deep breath. "Thank you," she says quickly, and I can tell how much it cost her to say that.

Jetta doesn't trust easily, she's blunt, and she's prideful. So the fact that she's extending her gratitude to Hugo says a lot. He nods in return, and she continues on her way, the guys following behind her.

When Hugo and I are alone, he relaxes back and loses the tough alpha look as he runs a hand over his face. I like that he feels comfortable enough with me that he can be himself, minus the alpha title. "Give it to me straight. How bad is her troupe master?"

I blow out a breath and shake my head. "I only saw him that one time, but from what I could tell, and what Jetta told me...he's not a good enemy to have. I'm not even sure what kind of Cane he is. I don't think he's a shifter."

Hugo groans. "He's not a fucking vampire, is he?"

My alpha isn't so fond of vampires.

I shake my head. "I don't think so."

Hugo nods and taps his finger against the desk in thought. "Do you trust her?"

"I only spent three days with her when I was fourteen," I answer honestly. "But...she was the first shifter to ever act like a friend. She's strong, and she doesn't take any shit, and I didn't know her long, but she left an impression on me. It might sound weird, but yeah, I trust her."

He nods at my words. "There are two things you always trust. Your gut, and your animal," Hugo says, holding up two fingers.

"Yeah, well, my animal mated with three shifters who don't want me, so what does she know?" I mutter.

Hugo grunts something unintelligible. "You could invite her to join our pack."

I blink at him in surprise. Hugo always keeps his doors open to shifters who feel like they don't belong anywhere, but it's always done carefully. He usually invites them to stay as a guest for a few weeks while the pack gets to know the shifter, before he offers to become their alpha. He likes to make sure he knows their character before inviting them to become one of us.

"You'd invite her? Just like that?"

"No, I'm saying *you* can invite her. I trust your judgment. Whatever you decide, I'll support."

His words mean more to me than I can admit, and I won't take this responsibility lightly. "I'll get to know her again, just to make sure. But I think she'd be a great addition. She could fit in well here. Besides, she has nowhere else to go, and being a rogue while her troupe master is after her won't be easy," I tell him. "You sure you'd be okay with having that heat brought down on us? If he finds out that she's joined our pack, he could press charges."

Hugo lifts a shoulder. "He could try, but even though collaring shifters is legal, it's frowned upon. And I won't technically be breaking any laws."

"You won't?"

He shakes his head. "Her collar is gonna fall off all by itself. Nothing against the law about that," he says with a cunning grin. "Also nothing against the law with her joining—as an uncollared shifter."

I laugh and shake my head. "You cat shifters are so sly."

"And you duck shifters are flighty," he says, changing the topic. "You can't avoid them, Addie." He wheels his chair closer to the desk so he can lean his forearms against the top. "You have to meet up with them and talk."

I blow out a breath. "They know what pack I'm in. They could've contacted me anytime, but they didn't. That gives me my answer."

"Severing all three bonds at the same time could kill you," he says, not pulling any punches.

"It won't," I say with far more confidence than I feel. "Trust me, I don't want to be miserable, and I definitely don't want to die. I'm not a martyr. But I'll be fine."

"You don't know that. I've known shifters who have died after a single mate bond was severed. Need I remind you that you have *three?*"

"Yeah, but those bonds had probably been formed for years, or at least months. Mine has only been activated for a week. It'll be fine. After a bit, the bond will break, and we can all move on. It's for the best."

He looks at me dubiously. "You're a stubborn duck."

"Yup."

He shakes his head and waves a hand toward the door. "Alright, get going. Take care of Jetta and see that our packmates don't swarm her."

I get to my feet with a chuckle. "Don't worry. Jetta can take care of herself."

Hugo grunts and starts pulling out papers to go over. "Yeah. Just make sure you do the same. If the pain gets worse, you call me. That's an order from your alpha," he says sternly.

I salute him before slipping out of the office, his words trailing behind me. I'm determined to do exactly that— take care of myself. So that's what I'll do. I'll get through this, just like I've gotten through everything else.

I don't need three preds who don't want me, and I refuse to live in a loveless—hell even a *like*-less—bond.

I steel myself for the days to come, knowing it won't be easy, but at least now with Jetta here, I'll have some distraction. Especially since the pain in my chest continues to twinge with every breath I take. I let out a shaky breath cursing at how much it tingles.

My mates really ducking suck.

I really hope Hugo isn't right about breaking these bonds. But to be honest, I'm surprised it hurts as much as it does. We were only together for a single night. I've never heard of a bond being this strong so soon. But maybe that's because I have three of them instead of one. At least, that's the only reason I let myself think of right now.

The other option is that our bonds are solid because

they're my perfect mates, but I can't go there. I can't think about that. It'll just make their rejection even worse.

I force myself to walk back to the warehouse without scratching at the spot on my chest. Maybe if I don't acknowledge the pain, it won't be so bad. I'm a big fan of ignoring problems. I'm also a big fan of living. So if severing these mate bonds starts to kill me, I'm gonna sever something of *theirs* that they're big fans of.

Their dicks. I'm gonna sever their dicks.

13

LAFE

We are such dicks.

We just let her leave, and none of us even tried to stop her.

It's been a week since Addie walked out, and the bad feeling in my chest has only gotten worse. Herrick insisted that the bond would crack open easier than an egg because it isn't real, but so far, he's been dead fucking wrong. For only having been together for a short amount of time, our bond has proved to be shockingly strong, and my animal isn't giving her up easily. If anything, he's digging in even harder with his teeth *and* his claws.

The second Addie walked out the door, my coyote started whining at me, pacing under my skin like a juvenile pup. And I'm not the only one who's been affected. Penn and Herrick have been growling, grumpy sons of bitches too. Well, more than usual, I mean.

I hear the front door open and slam shut, and I look up

from my spot on the couch to see Herrick stalk inside. He has a tank and board shorts on, which are noticeably wet. I cock a brown brow at him. "You went to the lake again?"

He ignores my question and continues past me to go to the kitchen where he grabs a bottled water and starts chugging it.

"You're such a fucking asshole," I mutter under my breath.

Of course, he catches my words because of his shifter hearing, and he spins around to glower at me. "We got a problem?" he challenges.

Anger and frustration ripple over me, but I give him a smart ass smirk because I know it'll irritate the shit out of him. "A problem?" I ask, with mock nonchalance. "Why would we have a problem? You just made our mate feel like shit as soon as she revealed her animal, and then you've spent the last week trying to convincing us that our bond with her isn't real, but we both know that's bullshit by now, don't we? Yet you still won't admit it, because like I said, you're a *fucking asshole*. So yeah, I guess we do have a problem."

He opens his mouth to argue, but then closes it again and curses under his breath. He brings a hand up and rubs it over his scalp in frustration. He tosses his empty water bottle in the trash can, and I sigh and lean my head back on the couch cushion, my eyes locked on the ceiling.

We don't talk for a few minutes, and the only sound is the game playing on the TV. Tension has been high, particularly between Herrick and me. I want him to admit that he's wrong, but he keeps waiting to be right. I know him, though. Herrick isn't a bad dude, but he is a stubborn son of a bitch. But even he knows by now that he was wrong about our bond. And every day that he continues to fight it makes me even more pissed at him.

We've been best friends since we were pups, and the three of us were put into training to become pack enforcers when we were ten. We've watched each other's back and fought side by side ever since, so this strain between us isn't familiar. He's always been a grumpy asshole, but I've never resented him before, and I don't want this anger to be the beginning of the end of our friendship.

"This isn't gonna let up," I point out.

He knows I'm right, because the mate-call hounds us constantly. It pushes us to go to Addie every second of every day. And nights? Nights are even fucking *worse*. It feels wholly unnatural to be apart from her.

Usually, when shifters bond, they sequester themselves away for a few weeks until that bond is solidified. Being separated from her so soon is like being constantly starved and edgy, with a pain in the chest that won't go away.

Not to mention the fucking horniness. That hasn't eased up *at all*. I'm not even in a rut anymore, but every time I catch Addie's scent somewhere in the house, my dick thinks it's go-time.

"So. Was she there?" I finally ask, my gaze still on the ceiling.

"...No."

His answer is quiet and abject, and it's the closest he's ever come to admitting that he misses her too. He's been going to the Blackmuck Lake every single day, which was where he first met her.

Penn and I know it's his way of looking for her—for seeking a way to reconcile—but she hasn't gone back there. Out of the corner of my eye, I catch him rubbing the spot on his chest where the relentless tug won't quit, and just like that, my anger deflates out of me.

"The mate-call hasn't let up," he says, sounding equally surprised and frustrated.

I pick up my head to glance over at him. "And it's not going to," I reply with a shrug. I lean forward and rest my forearms on my knees. "I saw your coyote last night."

He shoots me a look. "I was just tracking *your* coyote."

I scoff. "Bullshit."

He doesn't try to argue further, because he knows his lie is weak as fuck. He went to Addie's pack land last night, just like I did—just like I have been every night. After the third day of being separated from Addie, I couldn't resist the mate-call anymore. The hook inside of my chest kept tugging, and I swear, my cock turned into a compass, trying to point me in her direction.

So I waited until Herrick and Penn went to their rooms for the night, and I let my coyote come out. As soon as I'd shifted, my animal took off, tracing Addie's scent all the way back to the huge-ass territory on the outskirts of town where she and her pack live.

It took my coyote a good twenty minutes to get there, and it was impressive. The Aberrant pack land is protected by a tall fence, a guarded gate, lookout points, and a ton of security cameras. I didn't want to risk being caught, so my coyote didn't get too close, but even being in her air space seemed to calm my animal down, at least a little bit.

I've gone back every night since then. When my coyote isn't pacing around the perimeter, he'll watch a particular part of the fence for hours on end. He's probably hoping that if he stays at that spot long enough, our mate will sense him and come walking out.

But maybe the mate-call isn't as strong for her, because I haven't seen her once, much to my disappointment. The second night, Penn's coyote followed me. Last night, Herrick finally joined us. But it hadn't made any difference, because Addie hadn't shown herself to us.

I didn't like the thought that she wasn't being called to us the same way we were being called to her. I had hoped that her animal would be driving her just as crazy as ours were, but it didn't seem like that was the case. As far as I could tell, she had gone to her pack's land and stayed there to ride out the rest of her wave, and hadn't ventured out once.

The thought of her being around other males right now, even just her packmates, is almost enough to make me accidentally shift on the spot and start pissing everywhere to mark my territory. And make no mistake, as far as my coyote is concerned, Addie *is* my territory. The bond instincts are forceful as fuck, heightening the feelings of possessiveness that I know we haven't earned.

And it's true—we haven't earned shit when it comes to Addie. Our animals answered her call and we'd all bitten her to taste her blood, but aside from that, we've done nothing. *I've* done nothing. What I should've done was drag her back inside that day and forced us all to talk rationally without arguing. Or maybe I should've just dragged her back to my room and finished what we'd started earlier. My dick liked that option.

But I hadn't done shit, because Herrick had gone on and on about how we didn't know her, how a duck wasn't a suitable mate for a coyote, and how she couldn't possibly handle all three of us, anyway. Even Penn, who was usually good at being level-headed and not rushing into anything, had been silenced by him.

So when I saw Penn and Herrick's coyotes at Addie's territory too, things changed. If the call was too strong even for them to resist, then I knew Herrick had to be wrong. Our animals are digging in instead of retreating, and that fact alone lets me know that this isn't an accidental thing brought on by just sex or over-eager animals. There's something deeper going on here.

I trust my animal, and if he decided to choose Addie as his mate, then who the fuck am I to doubt him? Besides, one of the reasons we left our old pack was to find mates.

Granted, we didn't exactly expect for all of us to choose the same one, but...hey, it's not like we haven't shared before. And just because she isn't what we expected, doesn't mean that she isn't worthy.

I'm pissed at myself that I let her walk away and that I

played any part in her being hurt. I'm going to hate myself forever if I don't fix this. But maybe, with how Herrick is acting today, I won't have to worry about choosing her or them. Maybe we can still salvage this.

I have hope that they want to. Penn found Addie's old phone under the seat of the car the day after our fight. He slipped it into his pocket, and I haven't seen it since. Nosy son of a bitch probably went through her pictures and messages. And yeah, I wanted to go through it, too. I want to know everything about her. The only thing stopping me from asking to see her phone was that I was positive he wouldn't give it to me. He might hide it better, but he's feeling just as possessive of her as I am.

"Ready?"

I look over at Penn as he comes walking into the living room.

"No," I say tersely.

Penn shoots me a look and runs a frustrated hand through his blond hair. "We have to join a pack, Lafe, and we already had this meeting set up. We can't back out now or it'll look bad. Besides, this is just a meet and greet."

He knows I don't agree with going through with our application to join Pack Rockhead. Penn and Herrick might doubt that they're the ones responsible for attacking Addie, but I believe her.

"Come on, or we're gonna be late," Penn says.

Part of me wants to say fuck this and refuse to go. But we've acted as our own mini-pack since we were kids. We made an oath to each other a long time ago to stick together. So that's what I've been doing. Sticking with them. But I'm only biding my time, waiting for them to pull their heads out of their asses and realize that Addie is exactly what we need.

"I don't want any part of this. I've been patient. I've listened to your fucking side," I tell Herrick. "I'm not joining a pack that our mate hates."

Penn and Herrick share a look that instantly makes me go on alert. "What?"

"Look, we heard what you said. You think Addie was right about Pack Rockhead. Which is another reason why we're going."

"What do you mean?"

"Well...I was there that day at the bank robbery. I might recognize a scent or see someone. Addie believes it was them, and you believe Addie, so…" he trails off, looking at me expectantly.

"So you're actually going to see if we can find anything out?" I ask, flabbergasted.

Penn shrugs. "Yeah. We were obviously wrong about the bond. So maybe we're wrong about this too."

I get to my feet with a clap. "Ducking hell, *finally!* Took you assholes long enough."

"Yeah, well, she probably wants nothing to do with us now. But maybe if we can find out something for her…"

I grin. *"Oh.* So you're gonna bribe her with info on Pack Rockhead so that she'll talk to us again?"

Penn looks a bit sheepish but doesn't deny it. "You got any better ideas?"

"Nope," I say, clapping him on the shoulder as we walk out. "Lead the way, boss."

"Fuck off."

My grin just gets wider. Penn is our unofficial leader, so he's always throwing his weight around and getting the last word, but he hates when I call him boss.

"They could still be innocent," Herrick points out on our way to the car. "There's no harm in meeting them."

I shake my head at him because that's just it. There's *plenty* of harm in it. We might be meeting with the pack who attacked Addie, and if that's the case, my mate bond instincts might go berserk.

We're quiet on the drive, no doubt thinking about all the implications of what we might be walking into, but a thought comes to me. "I think Addie has a history with Pack Rockhead."

Penn glances at me from the rearview mirror. "What makes you say that?"

"That day when her alpha showed up, they were talking about it. I don't know, it's just the impression I got. She seemed...scared." I catch Herrick curling his fingers into fists and I consider my next words carefully. "Listen, I've thought about this a lot, and I decided I'm going to go see her. Apologize. I don't want to let the bond sever. If she'll have me, I'm gonna try this out, and I think you should too."

Both of them go still. "We don't even know her," Herrick argues lamely.

"She doesn't want us," Penn adds.

I snort. "Are you seriously using that as an excuse to be a stubborn son of a bitch? She said all of that because she was hurt and pissed. Hell, I would've said that, too. She'll change her mind once you're actually nice to her. Or...maybe it'll just *fly* over her head," I add with a smirk.

Penn looks at me warily. "You're gonna say a lot of duck puns aren't you?"

"Yep."

"But we're coyotes," Herrick puts in. "We can't be mated to a—"

I punch him on the arm, *hard*, cutting off his words. He whirls around, nostrils flaring, but I point a finger in his face before he can respond. "That's bullshit prejudice you're spewing. You're better than that. Sure, it's not the norm for preds and preys to mate, but so what? Our animals are intelligent and instinctual," I remind him. "You trust your coyote and he always leads you right. Maybe you should trust him now when it comes to a mate. Does it really bother you that much that she's a duck?"

"Yeah," he grits out. Then, "No. Fuck, I don't know!" He

turns his back on me again to glare out the window. "That shit was never done in our old pack."

"Well, we aren't in our old pack, are we?" I shoot back.

"Guess not."

"We left for a reason, Herrick," I remind him. "Because we realized that some shifters, especially huge pred packs like ours, are stuck in their ways. We were caught in centuries-old rules and expectations. It was all politics and power plays. We wanted something different, remember?"

"Yeah. Yeah, I remember."

I finally feel like I'm getting somewhere. "Okay, then. Now look me in the eye and tell me you don't like her, regardless of her animal." He doesn't say a thing. "Exactly. You do like her. And your animal *definitely* digs her, or he wouldn't have answered the mate-call in the first place, or be sitting outside her compound at night. I'm gonna apologize and ask her out. You should, too. Both of you. Our animals formed a quad bond and we should see it through."

After a moment of heavy silence, Herrick sighs. *"Fuck.* I was a dick."

"Yep. But we can still fix this."

Herrick arches a brow. "Really?" he drawls.

"Eh, maybe."

Herrick shakes his head, but the corner of his mouth tilts up.

"She's our mate. She's worth the effort of trying. The worst that can happen is she rejects us, which we already did to *her*. If that happens, we'll go our separate ways, same way we're doing now. But at least we'll know we tried. We owe it to her and to ourselves to apologize and try to fix this."

He looks back at me, his expression unreadable. "When did you get so fucking wise?"

I try to contain my cocky grin. "Probably around the time you grew into a giant asshole."

He tosses an empty bottle of water at me, but I dodge it with a laugh.

"So we all agree, then? We're doing this whole quad mate thing with Addie?" Penn asks, stealing looks at us.

"Hell yes, we're doing it." And hopefully doing *her* again soon, too.

Relief washes over his expression. "Okay. Then we go talk to her after this. Agreed?"

Herrick and I both nod, and a huge weight lifts off my chest. Anticipation starts growling in my stomach, ready to be reunited with our mate. *Our* mate. It seems surreal, and yet, the three of us have always been so close that it feels right.

"Okay, then we'll get this meeting over with and we'll see if we can find anything out. If they did hurt Addie, then they're gonna have a fucking big problem with us. But we can't act suspicious. We'll have to tell them we're still deciding on which pack to join, and after the meeting, we'll get the hell out of there."

"And then we go talk to Addie," I add.

They both nod in agreement. *Thank fuck.* My coyote is practically yipping in excitement.

The meeting place is at a motorcycle bar in town called *Rev's*. When Penn pulls up to it, we see motorcycles lining up the dirt parking lot, and I can hear rock music and laughter spill from the open door. There are two shifters standing at the entrance, acting as bouncers. We exchange one more look before getting out of the car and making our way towards the entrance.

One of the shifters wearing steel-toed boots and a wife beater spits at the ground as we walk up. "State your business."

"We're here to meet with Curb," Penn saying, stopping in front of him.

I snort under my breath at his name. The bouncers both narrow their eyes on me. "Somethin' funny?"

I open my mouth, but Herrick puts a hand against my chest to cut off my sarcastic reply. "You gonna let us in, or are we gonna have a problem?" He looks them dead in the eye, practically begging to start shit. Instead, the bouncers smirk and jerk their heads at us to go inside. "Curb's at the bar."

We pass the bouncers and make our way inside the dark and hazy space that smells of cigarettes, sex, pot, and booze. The place is filled with Rockhead shifters and some humans, too.

The building is all wood panelling and faded leather booths, with pool tables and a bored DJ at the back. My eyes shoot up in surprise when we pass a naked woman lying on top of a table. Her fake tits are on display and there are four guys sitting at the booth around her. They're stacking empty beer bottles on top of her and laughing as she tries not to move. My eye ticks in disgust at the lewd words coming out of their mouths.

One of them fondles her breast while another shoves an empty beer bottle in between her lips. "Open up nice and wide, sugar," he tells her as he pushes the bottle into her mouth. "If you're a good girl and don't let it fall, you can have my dick in there instead." The other guys chuckle darkly, and my blood boils when I see her hands tremble, not in anticipation, but in fear. The scent of her distress is unmistakable. She's a human, and the fact that they're disrespecting any female like this, shifter or not, makes me furious.

A low growl sounds out, but to my surprise, the noise doesn't come from me. I look over and see Penn's face is about three shades darker. The veins in his arms are pulsing menacingly as he clutches his fists hard enough to break bones.

The guys at the booth look over and eye us. One of them takes a swig of his beer before tossing it across the bar, letting it shatter on the floor. The girl flinches. "Who the fuck are you?"

"We're here to meet with Curb," Herrick answers.

We're attracting all sorts of looks, but the man lifts his chin and looks over our shoulders. "Curb! New pups are here."

Herrick and Penn bristle but don't say anything. I can tell they're both about a word away from throwing some fists. One surefire way to insult us is by calling a grown ass shifter a *pup*. Herrick's ears are practically steaming.

We turn around at the sound of footsteps and find Curb, the man of the hour, stalking toward us. He's a grizzly old fucker, with bushy gray eyebrows and tattoos spreading from his neck to his fingers. "You the ones who applied to join the pack?" he asks, looking us up and down.

Penn nods tersely.

"I'm Curb. The alpha's third. Take a seat," he says, indicating an empty table by the bar.

The four of us slide into chairs as a waitress immediately comes over and plops four beers in front of us. Herrick slams back half of his before I've even lifted my bottle.

"So, you've drifted this way and you're lookin' to join a new pack?" Curb asks.

Herrick steals a look at Penn, but it's clear that he's still preoccupied with the distressed naked chick on the table behind us, so Herrick takes over. "Yeah. We're ready to settle back into a pack, and we're looking at our options."

Curb wipes the beer froth from his mouth with the back of his arm. "Options?" he laughs. "Son, unless you want to join a pack of pussy misfit freaks of nature, we're the only ones around here, and we're a damn strong pack."

Pussy misfit freaks? My fingers curl around the neck of my beer bottle in anger.

"Yeah, we heard about Pack Aberrant," Herrick says carefully. He shoots me a look, telling me with his expression to calm the fuck down.

Curb cackles again, oblivious. "Yep. An embarrassment to all pred shifters everywhere. My alpha has been petitioning to get their pack dissolved. It ain't right, havin' a bunch of deformed and weak freaks with their own pack. They should be rogues like they're meant to be. Picked off by the stronger packs."

"That's a bit harsh."

Curb shrugs. "It's natural. Prey shifters and fucked up outcasts shouldn't be breeding. We don't need that shit spreading in our genes."

Red. All I'm seeing is red. The vein in Penn's neck looks about ready to burst, and the assholes behind us are still fucking with that girl. My entire body is tense, every noise and smell furthering my disgust. If this is what a strong alpha pred pack looks like, I want nothing to do with it.

When the girl makes a noise, we all glance over to see that one of the shifters has gotten to his feet and is unbuckling his belt. "Good job, sugar," he tells her, aiming to take her right then and there on the table while the other guys watch, while continuing to balance beer bottles on her naked body.

Curb notices the direction of our gazes and smirks at the display. "If you join us, that's just one of the perks. Human whores to fuck and pred females to mate."

Penn jumps to his feet like he's going to punch the guy, but I quickly shove my bottle into his chest. "Good idea, bro. Go get me another one, too."

Penn's head whips over to look at me, nostrils flaring and eyes lit up with fury. I press my bottle harder into his chest and give the smallest of head shakes. "Get Herrick one too, will ya?"

Penn hesitates for another second, and then turns and storms toward the bar.

Fuck, that was close.

The last thing we need is to start a fight in the middle of their pack bar. We're outnumbered and we'd have our asses handed to us in a second. Plus, we still need to find out information, and we can't do that with fists.

Herrick and I exchange a look, and he clears his throat. "What about non-preds?"

Curb laughs. "Non-preds? None here."

I frown. "That's strange. I mean, I know pred-dominant packs usually mate with their own breeds and have pred offspring, but to not have *any* non-preds? That's unusual. What about other Cane breeds? Some of your shifters must be mated to other types of Canes? Witches, vampires…?"

"Forming a mate bond outside our shifter breed is against Pack Rockhead law. Humans *or* other Canes—it's forbidden. And as for our shifters having non-pred offspring…I didn't say we've never had 'em. I said there's none here," he says cryptically.

"Meaning?"

"Meaning we cut 'em loose or…" he shrugs. "The problem corrects itself with the yearly challenges."

I blanche. "Are you saying that you challenge non-preds that are born into your pack? You challenge *kids?*"

Curb shrugs. "We're a pure pred pack. It's the way it's always been. Once a non-pred shifter comes of age, they can either face the challenge, or they can walk."

I can't believe what I'm hearing. What he's saying is unheard of. Sure, shifters favor preds, but to turn away our own young? That practice is barbaric and unnecessary. Nearly everyone from our old pack was a predator. But every once in a while, there were members who chose to mate outside of the norm, and take up with a witch or a non-pred, or hell, even a human. It wasn't illegal, just frowned upon.

Even so, the children of those unions were never given the ultimatum to fight to the death or go rogue. The fact that Rockhead has done this for centuries makes the acid in my stomach churn and boil.

Curb's obvious disdain for any kind of shifter other than a

predator shows me exactly what we could become if we let prejudice rule us. When I steal a look at Herrick, I can tell from the horrified expression on his face that his train of thought is the same as mine. No wonder Addie looked at us with such contempt. We were acting no better than Curb.

That thought *really* makes me sick when Curb pinches the thigh of one of the waitresses that walks by and pulls her in so that he can stick his hand up her skirt. She flinches, but stands stock-still until he laughs at her discomfort and smacks her on the ass. "Go on. Those beers ain't gonna serve themselves." The human female flees as quickly as she can without running.

Behind us, the shifter is pounding into the naked female on the table, causing lewd noises to fill the air. I've never wanted to leave a place as much as I wish I could walk out of here right now.

"So, first thing's first," Curb says, clapping his hands together and redirecting our gazes. "What kind of animals are you boys?"

"Coyotes," Penn says, coming back up and setting more beers on the table. I take one and pretend to drink from it, but I'm too pissed off to swallow anything down.

Curb nods, obviously pleased. "Coyotes. Shoulda guessed. We've got a couple of those. Wolves and bears, few mountain lions. Bobcats, too. You should fit right in," he says, picking at his teeth with his long fingernail. "If you get in, you'd be coming in at the bottom of the pack, but you'll have the chance to work your way up in rank. You'll all have to prove yourselves first, though, before we'll take your application to join seriously. You'll have to complete a task to show your loyalty and demonstrate your strength before we'll accept you into Rockhead." His eyes light up when a thought comes to him. "Come to think of it, I might have the perfect task."

"What's that?" Penn asks.

Curb looks around the bar, and when he spots who he's looking for, he hollers, "Hey, Drag! Get your ass over here!"

I watch as a big, bald, ugly motherfucker stops his game at the pool table and comes striding over. "Yeah, Curb?"

Curb nods at us. "New recruits. I want you to use them to help you with that bitch, Addie."

All three of us tense. Blood pounds in my ears enough to drown out the exhibitionistic sex still going on behind me. Addie was right. They attacked her, and they're going to try it again. My coyote growls inside of me, and it takes every ounce of willpower I have not to shift. If I lose control, Curb will know something set me off, and the last thing I want is for him to have the upper hand. Every drive inside of me is now focused on one thing— protecting Addie.

Drag looks us over with consideration. "Yeah? That might work. She don't know them."

"Exactly," Curb says with a nod.

I open my mouth to question him, but Penn stops me by speaking up first. "What's the story on her?" he asks, his tone even and steady despite the hard lines around his eyes.

Drag sneers. "The bitch needs to be put in her place."

Herrick's hands grip the edge of his chair hard enough to splinter it.

"Oh, yeah? What for?" Penn asks nonchalantly.

"Let's just say she stepped over the line and disrupted a job," Curb answers vaguely.

Drag snorts. "She did more than that. It put a taint on our whole damn pack when the bitch was born. No surprise that she ran off when she came of age. She always was a weak little freak. Too bad, I would've liked to have taught her a lesson or two in the challenge ring," he says with a sick smirk on his face. "But we all knew that she'd fly away like a fuckin' coward. That's what prey do. They run from us preds. That's what makes them prey."

"At least now you have a chance to chase her again," Curb says with a laugh, clapping Drag on the shoulder.

Drag's eyes light up like that's the best news he's had in months. But my mind is stuck on one word. *Again.* Apparently, I'm not the only one.

"Again?" Herrick asks. "You've had problems with this female before?"

"Remember the yearly challenges we have for the shifters that come of age?" Curb replies. "Well, Aderyn Locke was one of those. A prey born in our pack. She had no place here, and she knew it. She refused the challenge and decided to run, of course. No fuckin' surprise there, although Drag here was sore as shit about it," he says, cackling when he sees Drag's pissed off face. "She joined up with those misfit freaks. Fits right in with them."

"But now she's fucking with Rockhead's rep again and messin' up our jobs. I finally got the okay from Alpha Rourn to teach her a lesson," Drag says with malicious glee. "Been a long time comin'."

It takes everything in me not to launch myself across the table and start pummeling him. I hadn't gotten a look at the fucker that attacked Addie outside the motel that day, but this is him. I can feel it. He's out for her blood—and maybe more. *Over my dead fucking body.* My coyote snarls inside of me.

"What do you want us to do?" I hear Herrick say. I have no idea how he's still able to keep his cool right now.

"Simple," Curb says with a shrug. "You'll go with Drag to bring her in. She won't recognize you, so we'll have a better shot this time. Shouldn't be any problem with three of you and one of her. She's a fuckin' bird for chrissakes."

"And what are you doing with her once you have her?" Penn asks.

"Well, we've gotta set an example don't we? No one fucks with Rockhead's business, and just because she was born in our pack, doesn't mean she can get away with shit like this. Alpha Rourn will remind her to respect her betters."

This fucker.

Behind us, the shifter grunts with his finishing thrust, and the others around him clink their glasses in celebration and laugh when the last of the bottles fall off the girl's body. I dig my nails into my thighs to keep from turning around. We need to get the fuck out of here before one of us snaps.

"Just tell us the time and place," Herrick says as he takes another swig of beer. If it weren't for his tense shoulders, I wouldn't be able to tell how on edge he really is. Meanwhile, I'm sure that my eyeballs are about to burn holes into Drag's skull.

Curb glances at Drag. "She left the compound yet?"

Drag scratches his chin and shakes his head. "Not that I've heard, but I've been havin' Riot track her. I'll give him a call and see if she's surfaced. She's gotta leave the nest sometime."

Curb nods at him and then looks back at us. "Well, there you go boys. Give Drag here your number and be ready to leave as soon as he contacts you. You help us take down this female, and I'll personally hand over your application to Alpha Rourn to be admitted into our pack. You'll be a good addition to Rockhead. The Moon Pack you came from is one of the best, I hear."

"Yep," Penn says simply.

"Any questions?"

"Nope, I think we get the gist of it," I say dryly. Herrick and Penn both shoot me a look, but I just couldn't stop myself.

Curb's eyes fall to me. "What's that, pretty boy? You gonna have a problem with following orders?"

I clench my teeth but manage to shake my head. "No."

Curb snorts. "What's the problem? Gettin' cold feet already because she's a female? Maybe you three aren't as capable as I thought you were."

Penn leans back in his chair confidently. "Don't worry. We'll take care of her."

I barely contain my snort. Too bad for Curb that Penn doesn't mean that in the way that he thinks.

"Fine. Now get on out of here," he says, already eyeing another one of the waitresses who passes us by with a tray full of shots.

We all get up and leave without another word. When I look over at the booth, the naked female is now sitting on the booth on the shifter's lap, obviously glad to be off the table. When she catches us looking, she gives us a sneer and quickly looks away, like the last thing that she wants is for anyone else to look at her. I don't blame her.

Once we're outside, I let out the breath I had been holding, but none of us speak as we make our way to our car. I take the back as Penn drives and Herrick gets in the front. We slam our doors at the same time and Penn starts the car and starts taking off before the engine even turns all the way over.

When we're about to turn out of the lot, a car catches my eye and I lean forward, slapping my hand against Penn's arm. "There's the human—Mario. He's the fucker who took her on that date. He was the one following us when I got Addie on my motorcycle."

Herrick growls and we all watch as he pulls into the bar parking lot and gets out. Penn starts to put the car in park, but Herrick stops him. "Not here. Not now."

"Fuck this shit."

"Herrick's right," I say, as much as I don't want to. "We need to leave."

"Those fuckers are after our mate," Penn says through clenched teeth.

I exchange a look with Herrick. If Penn loses his shit and gets out of this car, this will not end well for any of us. "We can't start shit here, Penn. We'll get our asses handed to us and we won't be able to warn Addie. We gotta leave. For Addie."

That seem to snap him out of his rage long enough to blink and look over at us. I can see that the bond that drives his protective instincts is shifting away from imminent attack to strategic planning. The last thing his coyote wants is for any of his actions to hurt Addie.

"Fine. But we make that fucker pay," Penn says with a snarl.

"We will," Herrick promises darkly.

Penn throws the car back into drive and rushes out of the lot, our tires screeching on the asphalt as we make it onto the highway. We all take several minutes to think in silence, our brains soaking up everything that went down and what it means for us and for Addie.

I'm the first one to break the tense silence. "This is not good."

"No shit. They're after our mate, and I fucking called her a liar. And that was *after* I told her she wasn't good enough for us. Obviously it's not fucking good, Lafe!"

"Hey, don't get mad at me," I tell him. "You're the one with the automatic asshole setting."

"Fuck!" Herrick punches his fist against the dashboard, earning him a glare from Penn. "What am I gonna do? Addie is gonna hate us more than she already does. We should've listened to her. *I* should've listened to her."

"Yeah, you should've. But it's not too late, bro. We can fix this. We're still bonded to her, thank fuck."

"She doesn't want to be."

"Then we'll have to change her mind."

Herrick runs his hands over his scalp in frustration. "Okay, okay. We need a plan."

Penn nods in agreement. "We have to play this right. We need to protect her, but we also don't want to start a pack war, because that could be devastating. If they're after her, we need to stop it, but if we make things worse, then Rockhead could attack Aberrant, and we don't want that happening. Rockhead are a pack of dirty fuckers. The last thing we want is them attacking her pack and killing her packmates."

"We won't let them hurt her," I growl, my animal angry at the thought.

"Of course not."

"So? What are we gonna do?"

"We're going to stop those Rockhead assholes from hurting our mate. We'll kill every last one of them if we have to." Penn shoots a sideways glance at Herrick. "But first, we have to get her to talk to us again."

I don't know which task sounds more daunting.

"How are we gonna do that?" Herrick asks. "She'll probably refuse to see us."

I smirk and slap him on the back. "Get ready to grovel, asshole."

14

HERRICK

Three hours after we leave the Rockhead meeting, Penn is driving us downtown to *Doggie Style Pet Shop*, where our mate now works, apparently. It's an embarrassing name, and Lafe giggles like a fucking girl every time one of us says it.

We got lucky finding out where she is from her friend, Zoey. Penn found her number on Addie's phone and called her on our way back from the Rockhead meeting. It took a few tries, but Zoey finally answered and we got her to tell us where we can find Addie. Penn did all the talking. He's a charming motherfucker when he wants to be.

"I just find it funny that a shifter mated to three coyotes works at a place called *Doggie Style*," Lafe snickers from the back.

"Yeah. So you've said. Three times," Penn replies dryly as he turns the car into the business mall lot.

As soon as he parks, he has to lock the doors to stop Lafe from jumping out. "Wait."

Lafe loses the happy-go-lucky look that's been on his face ever since we started driving in her direction. "Fuck that! I don't want to wait anymore. I've waited long enough for you fuckers to pull your tails out of your asses. I'm not waiting any longer to go see her. My coyote is fucking scraping me raw, man."

It's not an exaggeration. I feel the same way, and that's even with my denial and fighting my coyote every step of the way. Lafe has been for her since the beginning, so his instincts are probably even more heightened than mine.

"Chill," Penn tells him. "I'm not backing out. I'm telling you to wait because I think we should make Herrick go in first. Alone." He looks over at me with a shit-eating smirk.

I glower at him. "Why just me?"

"Because you're the one she's mostly pissed at," he says.

That's...that's accurate. Dammit.

"I don't think that's a good idea," I say, shaking my head as I steal looks over at the door to the pet shop. "She's probably super pissed. And a female coming down from her heatwave is already volatile and shit."

Penn's grin widens. "You're not scared, are you?" he taunts.

"Suck a dick."

"Just grow a pair and hurry up! I want to see her," Lafe says, pushing my arm. "And don't fuck this up," he adds.

I yank my arm away from his incessant pushing and glare at him over my shoulder. "Fine! But what the fuck am I supposed to say?"

Lafe shrugs. "You were an asshole about her animal. You made her and her duck feel *unworthy*. You have to fix that. Maybe use some duck-tape." He laughs at his own joke, and I roll my eyes.

"Yeah, I got that part, prick. I'm asking *how*. How do I fix it?"

Lafe's lip twitches. "Just *wing* it."

Fucking duck puns.

I move to slap him upside the head, but he laughs and dodges me.

"You're not fucking helping!"

"Okay, okay!" he says, trying to stop laughing as he holds his hands up in surrender. "Just apologize. Grovel. Beg. Do whatever you need to do to make things right with our *mate*," he says, emphasizing the last word. "Then convince her to give us another chance so that we can protect her from—" Lafe cuts off, his eyes caught on something out the window.

Penn and I swivel our heads to follow his gaze. My eyes instantly land on Addie coming out of the shop carrying a bag of garbage in her hands. She walks around the side of the building and tosses the bag in the dumpster at the end of the alleyway before turning around and walking back. Her hips swing with every step, and she looks so damn good, my dick instantly turns hard.

I curse under my breath. "What the fuck kind of uniform is *that?*"

Penn and Lafe are still staring at where she disappeared through the door, unable to answer me. Lafe is practically panting. I don't blame him. She's wearing a tight black skirt with suspenders over a white uniform shirt. The words, *"I Love Doggie Style...Pet Shop"* are printed on the front with the shop's logo underneath.

For fuck's sake. Not exactly subtle, is it?

"She has awesome tits," Lafe finally says, sounding pained.

"And ass," Penn adds.

I remember that ass bouncing on my dick during her heatwave. I remember those tits in my hands. "Dammit," I mutter under my breath as my cock continues to swell inside my pants. I have to adjust myself, and the guys snigger. "How am I supposed to talk to her when she looks like *that?*"

Lafe and Penn just laugh at my expense.

"Just take a quack at it," Lafe says.

This time, I do manage to smack him upside the head. It makes me feel a little better.

"Good luck, dude," Penn offers.

I grumble more expletives at them as I get out. I have a feeling this isn't going to go well, and having my ass handed to me while hard as a rock does not sound like a good time. I guess I deserve it.

———

Ten minutes later, I'm stomping back out to the car. My arms are full of stupid shit. I'm carrying three bags of merchandise, a dog bed, a kennel, and a huge fucking bag of kibble that I drop in the parking lot halfway to the car. I sigh when it explodes on the ground and kibble goes spilling out everywhere. Fuck it, the strays can have it.

I don't say a word as I throw open the back door and toss everything inside where Lafe is sitting, before slamming the door shut and then yanking open the front passenger door and climbing in.

"What is all this?" Lafe asks, pushing all of the the bags off of him so that they fall to the floor at his feet. He eyes a package of dog bones. "Did you talk to her?"

"Yeah, sort of," I deflect.

Penn frowns. "What does that mean? And you didn't answer Lafe. What is all this shit?" he asks, eyeing the kennel.

"I don't know, man!" I say, throwing up my arms. "One second, I'm trying to apologize and shit, and the next thing I know, she's selling me chew toys and a fucking muzzle."

Penn's lips twitch. "But...we don't have any pets," he points out unhelpfully.

"I know! It was her tits. Her tits looked fucking *awesome* in that uniform. And she was still pissed at me, so she kept cutting me off. Wouldn't let me talk. And then she just started selling me shit. Just kept piling it in my hands. Every time she bent over to pick something else up, I bought that shit too, because her ass *also* looked awesome. I couldn't stop it, man. It happened so fast. She said if I was gonna act like a dog, I might as well have the merchandise for it."

Lafe and Penn start howling with laughter.

"Shut the fuck up! I'd like to see one of you assholes try," I grumble. "She wouldn't listen to me. And she has a massive advantage with that uniform. Her suspenders stretched right over her nipples, for fuck's sake. They were hard the whole time."

"Obviously something else was hard, too," Lafe laughs.

I try to adjust myself in my pants again, but it's no use. I might as well have a fucking steel rod shoved down my pants. When she bent over that first time, I almost came right then and there.

Still laughing, Penn looks back at Lafe. "Alright, Lafe. You're up. She likes you."

But Lafe shakes his head. "No fucking way. I'm not fixing this for you. You guys were the assholes here, not me. *You* go in. Besides, if you're forced to buy stuff from her too, it won't make you go broke, Mister Money Bags. If I go in, she'll probably sell me a stallion or some shit. And she'll still be mad at you guys, so it'll solve nothing. We should all go in together."

Penn taps his hand against the steering wheel like he's

trying to gear himself up. "Okay, good point. We all go in then? United front."

I quickly nod. "We should've done that from the start."

Penn points at us, his face completely serious now. "No matter how great her tits and ass look, do not let her trick us into buying anymore shit."

Lafe and I nod solemnly. Her body is a real problem.

We follow him out of the car, making our way across the parking lot. Kibble crunches under our shoes as we walk, and Lafe has to contain a snicker. "Glad you think it's so funny."

"I'm just thoroughly enjoying that our ducking mate just handed you your pred ass." He looks way too happy about it.

Penn leads the way while Lafe and I follow behind. The door jingles when he swings it open, and we all pass through inside. The shop is small, but packed full of pet supplies, and smells assault us, mostly from the dog food and all the fish tanks. I'm embarrassed to admit that my coyote takes a longing look at the jerky strips by the counter.

"Addie, we need to talk—" Penn's words cut off because we round the corner of the aisle and find that she's bending over, her cute little ass pointed right at us.

She yelps and turns around, her hands flying to her butt as she yanks down her skirt. "Don't sneak up on me!"

She might've fixed her skirt so it's no longer riding up, but the damage has been done. She definitely wasn't bending over *that* far while I was in here earlier. I probably would've bought the whole damn store if she had been.

"Are you...wearing panties that say, 'Come here for a *howling* good time?'" Lafe asks, looking like this is the happiest moment of his life.

She blushes about ten shades of red and starts busying herself with hanging up more collars, looking anywhere but at us.

"Pretty sure that's a coyote pun, babe," Lafe says, looking downright giddy. "Is that a signal that you want us back?"

Her eyes flash to him. She has her hair braided, so her rainbow strands are mixing together with the blonde like an ice cream swirl. My coyote reminds me that he wants to lick her.

"Nope," she says, crossing her arms. "Coyotes aren't the only shifters that howl. In fact, I've heard that wolves do it better. I think I'll find out," she says, goading us. It works, because I'm already growling.

She barely finishes her sentence before Penn is on her. She lets out a little squeal of surprise, but doesn't stop him as he pins her against the shelf.

"What do you assholes want?" she asks, lifting her chin to Penn defiantly.

"You," Penn says as he grips her hips and leans in to run his nose along her neck.

I see her shiver, but she makes an effort to push him back,

so Penn drops his hands and steps away, even though I know it's gotta kill him to do it. Even now, I'm just itching to get closer to her. "Me?" she asks, with a humorless laugh. "Yeah, right."

"It's true," Lafe insists.

"Yeah? How's Pack Rockhead?" she taunts. "Heard you were spotted going toward Rev's, the biker bar that all the Rockhead's hang out in."

Damn. Word travels fast.

"It's true. We were there," Penn admits.

Her jaw grinds and her fists curl up. "Then get out."

"Addie—"

"No! I want you to leave. Now."

"Dammit, would you just listen?" I snap.

Her eyes flash to mine, but she's so stunned by my outburst that she actually does stop talking and listens to me. "You were right. They're assholes," I tell her. "We were wrong. *I* was wrong. Rockhead is nothing but a pack of scumbags doing shady shit, and they attacked you," I say, my voice nothing more than a growl.

"Now all of a sudden you believe me?" she asks, trying to sound incredulous, but I catch the slight waver of hope in her voice.

"That's right. And if you would've listened earlier, I would've explained and apologized, but you just kept shoving shit in my hands to buy."

She shrugs, completely remorseless. "I get paid commission on sales."

My lip twitches. Little minx. How the fuck did I ever think that she wasn't good enough for *me?* It's one-hundred-percent the other way around. I only hope that she hasn't realized that so that I still have a chance.

"Addie," Penn says, drawing back her attention to him. "We were wrong, and we were disrespectful assholes to you. Herrick most of all," he says.

I shoot him a glare. "Thanks a lot, fuckhead."

He just shrugs and continues.

"Listen, Addie, we—" Penn's words get cut off at the jingle of the bell above the door, and all four of our faces swivel over to an elderly human man holding a parakeet.

Lafe curses under his breath, and all three of us glower at the interruption. Bad fucking timing.

Addie quickly steps away from us and heads toward the front counter. As soon as the man spots her, he squints and starts shuffling forward.

Addie clears her throat to greet him. "How can I help you, sir?" Even though she's wearing a smile, I can tell she's nervous with all three of us watching her. Her fingers keep tapping against each other and her eyes dart over to us, like she needs to keep checking that we're still here.

The old man sidles up to the counter and slams an age-spotted hand onto the glass. "This here bird won't eat!

Pickiest little prick I ever saw," he tells her, glaring his milky eyes at the green and yellow bird.

"Oh. Okay," Addie says, looking over the bird. "What have you been feeding him?"

"I have one thing every single day," he says, holding up a spindly finger. "A tomato and mayo sandwich, yessir. But will Marty here eat it? *Oh no.* Not a shit bit. Steals my coffee sometimes, though. Found him swimming in my mug one morning, pleased as piss at himself."

The more he talks, the less Addie focuses on us. "Wait...what?" she asks, shaking her head like she heard him wrong.

"That's what I'm sayin'!" he explains. "Wastes perfectly good sandwiches!"

She fiddles with the suspender strap on her shoulder and gives the parakeet a commiserating glance. "Okie dokie...we will just...find some new food for you to try out. How does that sound?"

The old man grumbles something but waves her off in acceptance. Addie immediately rounds the counter and starts gathering seed treats and pellets, and then writes a list of fruits and vegetables the bird can have, too. I'm taking a guess that sandwiches and coffee are not on that list.

"All this for a damn bird," the man gripes on his way out, bag in hand and the parakeet still hanging out on his shoulder.

Addie shakes her head as the door swings shut. "He's

lucky that bird isn't a shifter. Probably would've done more than swim in his coffee."

Lafe chuckles, and then the three of us just stand awkwardly around the counter, trying to figure out how to navigate from here. She's self-conscious from our attention, and I hate that she feels like that. I know it's because of me.

Addie tugs on her braid and blows out a breath. "Look, guys, I'm glad you came down here and all, but I'm at work, and honestly? You had all week to contact me, but you didn't. Maybe our mate bond is strong, but that doesn't necessarily mean it's *right*. Maybe we should just...let it break."

All three of us stare at her, and I feel like I've just been sucker punched in the gut.

"No," Lafe says, shaking his head adamantly. "We're *not* doing that."

She sighs, and the sound breaks my fucking heart. "As much as the bond hurts when we're apart, I don't actually think it'll kill me, so—"

"Wait a fucking minute," Penn cuts in. "You've been in pain?"

She stops short and bites her lip, and it's obvious she hadn't meant to say that. "No. I mean, yes, but I can handle it."

"You should've told me," Lafe says, looking gutted. "Fuck, if I would've known…"

"Exactly," she cuts in. "I didn't want you to come to me because of that, or out of some hero complex. I won't have mates that are only with me out of a sense of duty."

"We don't—" Lafe begins.

"Stop! just stop," she says desperately, holding up her hands. "Please."

Color has bloomed on her cheeks and I can tell how hard she's trying to stay strong. My whole body is tense, because all I want to do is move the three steps forward it would take to stand in front of her and tug her against me. I want to fix this, but I don't know how. My coyote is clawing at me, hating her distress that he can sense.

"I'm glad that you all realize what kind of pack Rockhead really is, but that doesn't change anything. I'm a duck. You're coyotes. It would never work. Let's just let the bond break and you can forget all about me."

"Addie—"

"No, Lafe," she says, shaking her head and letting her hands tangle in front of her. "Can you guys please just go?" she asks, her face pointed at her feet. I know she's about two seconds away from crying, and I can't fucking stand it.

"We aren't leaving you. Not ever again."

Her blue eyes snap up to me, and for the second time, she's stunned into silence by my words. She studies my face like she's trying to burrow into my head and flip through the truth of my words. I let her see all of it. Every expression I have and how serious I am.

"Our animals answered your mate-call for a reason. It surprised the hell out of us, that's true. Predators hardly *ever* mate with prey. It took us off guard. Plus, the pack where we grew up...well, it just wasn't done there. But we realized what a huge mistake we made. Lafe knew all along, but Penn and I are stupid fucks apparently, because we couldn't see what was right in front of our eyes."

"Yeah? And what's that?" she asks.

"Our perfect mate."

She swallows hard and blinks faster, trying to hide the fact that her eyes are glossy. I can see that she's breathing faster, and she probably doesn't even know she's doing it, but her feet are inching closer to us as she comes back from around the counter.

"We're sorry, Addie," I tell her. "I'm so fucking sorry. Please give us another chance."

She takes a shaky breath and drags her eyes over all three of us. "You're...you're serious? You really want me as your mate?"

"If you'll have us," Lafe replies. "Although, these two are grumpy sons of bitches, I think you can take them."

She laughs, letting a quiet sob come out right alongside it. She swipes her hand under her eye and fidgets on her feet like she doesn't know what to do with herself. The guys and I exchange a look, communicating with each other silently. Lafe saunters over to the door and flicks the lock with a smirk.

"Hey, we aren't closed!" Addie hisses. "You can't just lock the doors."

"I'll make it up to the customers," Lafe promises. "Besides, this is more important."

"And what is *this,* exactly?"

Penn moves forward. "We might be doing things a little backwards here since we're already mated, but we want to date you. Get to know you," Penn says. "Let us make it up to you and give you the respect you deserve," he says, reaching for her again.

This time, she doesn't pull away from him. She lets his hand graze down her arm, and she shudders slightly at the touch. For some reason, my possessiveness doesn't include Penn or Lafe. Our quad bond is solid. If it were any other male touching her like that, I'd lose my shit.

"I'm so angry at you guys," she admits, and it fucking *kills* me when her voice cracks with emotion. "And I won't accept prejudiced pred assholes as mates. Not when they don't accept my duck or my pack," she tells us, forcing fire back into her words. "My duck is *me*. My pack is my family. And if you can't accept that…"

"We do," Penn says decisively.

She looks at him dubiously. "I've heard of mate bonds forming just for sex. Maybe—"

"This isn't just about the sex. I think we all know that by now. If that were the case, our bonds would've broken easily."

She casts us a look. "I guess so."

Lafe steps forward. "You're a kickass duck, and it's not just about the heatwave sex. Our coyotes are so attached, they've decided stalking your compound at night is a good pastime. That's something they'd only do for a true mate."

Her blonde brows shoot up in surprise. "You've been coming to Pack Aberrant land?"

"Yep."

She blows out a breath. Chews on her lips. Thinks.

"Let us make it up to you," Lafe repeats quietly. He starts trailing his hand up her other arm, while Penn reaches up and tugs off her hair tie. He pulls the strands loose so that he can thread his fingers through her long locks.

Her body is flushed and quivering from where her back is pressed against the counter. I can feel her mate-call rising up, reaching out to us, and our skin ripples as we try to suppress our shift.

Before she gives in, she bites her lip and looks over at me. I see her vulnerability, and it kills me to know that I put it there. I told her that she wasn't good enough for me, all because of cultural prejudices that I grew up with. But ever since she walked out on us, I've realized that none of that bullshit really matters.

I step up, taking up the middle between Penn and Lafe. I grab her jaw, letting my thumb brush along her neck. "Listen carefully, because I'm only gonna say this once. I'm still a predator. I don't beg, but I'm begging now," I tell her. "Please don't sever the bonds. I'm sorry. Give us another shot."

My heart beats a fucking mile a minute as I wait for her answer. Doubt crawls behind my eyeballs and claws at them, making them burn with pent-up emotion. I've never wanted something so much in my entire life as I want Addie to forgive me.

Instead of answering, she just watches me, and I'm pretty sure I blew the best thing that's happened to us. I don't even know if Penn and Lafe will be able to forgive me for it.

But then she swallows and her perfect lips part to speak. "Okay."

My eyes widen. "Okay?"

She smiles and nods. All three of us practically howl in relief. Okay is now the best fucking word in the world.

"But you assholes owe me big time," she says pointedly. "I'm talking epic dates. Multiple orgasms. Ice cream whenever I want it. And you have to swim in the lake with me," she demands.

Penn's lips twitch. "I think we can manage that."

Lafe leans in closer and grazes his lips against her neck. She tilts it to the side so he can have better access. "How many orgasms are we talking?" he asks, letting his teeth and tongue skim over her pebbling skin.

"At least three per sex session," she says breathily, barely able to keep her eyes open.

"Done," Lafe says, and he turns to look at us. "Let's make our little duck quack, shall we?"

I don't wait another second. I slam my lips down on hers. The second we make contact, our bond practically bursts forward and sings. My whole body shudders, my animal howling in triumph and lust when Addie moans into my mouth and grabs the back of my head to force me closer.

Penn has his hands all over her, sliding up her waist and collecting her breasts in his hands, making her moan even louder. Lafe continues to tease her neck, and my mouth drinks her in, my tongue demanding every inch of her.

"Do you forgive us for being assholes?" Penn asks.

I pull away, and smirk when she tries to chase my lips before answering.

"Your mate asked you a question," I tell her, letting my finger trail down her suspenders, pinching over the place where her nipple has pointed up at attention.

"I guess I'll forgive you," she says, her voice raspy with desire. "If you buy a few more things first."

Smirking at her smart ass, we all chuckle. "Whatever it takes, little duck. We want to do this thing."

"You mean you want to do *me,*" she corrects, taking in our hungry expressions.

"Yeah, that too," Lafe admits.

"Okay," she relents, licking her swollen lips. "But no lies. No happy ending bullshit. We can date and see where it goes." She holds out a hand. "Deal?"

Penn takes her hand, only to wrap it around the back of his neck. "Deal," he says, before leaning in to kiss her.

She makes a little whimpering noise as she melts against his chest, and the sound goes straight to my dick. Lafe reaches around and lifts up the back of her skirt and starts kneading her ass. When I see the front of her panties, I chuckle. "Wolves, my ass."

Penn pulls away at my words, and we all look down at the howling coyote on the front of her panties. Panties, I might add, that have a visible wet spot. I swipe my finger over them, and she moans. "Fine, yeah. I'm wearing coyote panties. I've also been using my vibrator all week because my mates are assholes," she says testily.

I'm pretty sure all three of us groan at that mental image. "That shit is going in the trash," I tell her.

"No ducking way," Lafe argues. "We're going to use it on her. Get her nice and wet for us," he says, letting his hand come forward to cup her mound. She whimpers again and angles toward him. "I'm going to love watching you come all over it, and then we're going feed you our cocks. How does that sound?" he asks, his fingers dancing over her clit.

"Yep, sounds good. Really super good," she pants.

I chuckle, but just before I can reach for her again, Penn's phone starts going off. He digs his hand into his pocket and reads the text, and his lips press together in a grim line from whatever he sees on the screen.

Dammit. Drag must already be contacting him.

Addie looks between us, noticing our change in demeanor. The haziness of lust starts to drain from her face. "What is it? What's wrong?"

Penn shoots off a reply text before stuffing his phone back into his pocket. He looks up at her again and sighs. "I'm sorry. This isn't how I wanted to get interrupted. I wanted the three of us to worship you for hours."

"I mean, yeah. That sounds like a good plan. Let's do that. Why can't we do that?" she asks quickly, looking vastly disappointed.

"We *are* going to do that. Just not right now. We have to put this on pause," Penn says, looking pained. Hell, he probably is. My dick is so hard it hurts. Addie looks just as put out. I grimace when I remember that she had to ride out the rest of her wave alone, when we should've been around to take care of her.

"Fine. But I will be cashing in this raincheck," she says pointedly. "Now, what's going on?"

"Pack Rockhead is coming after you."

Rather than look surprised or scared, she just snorts and fixes the strap of her suspender that slipped down. "Duh. Tell me something I don't know."

Her words take us off-guard and we all exchange a look. "You know?"

"Um, yeah. Their whole *attacking me at the motel thing* kind of tipped me off."

"They're out for blood. They blame you for the whole

bank fiasco and losing their payday. We played along, tried to get as much info as we could while we met with them. They decided that as part of our initiation into their pack, they'd use us to get you. An asshole named Drag just texted me our orders." He picks up the phone again and pulls up the text. "They know you're here at the shop, and they want us to bring you in."

"Motherducker," she says under her breath upon reading the text.

"They seem really pissed, like it's more than just the bank thing. It seems personal," Lafe puts in, fishing for info.

"That's because it is," she answers simply. "I was born into Pack Rockhead."

My eyes widen. *"What?"*

"Yep. My mother and step father are wolves. She had a secret affair that everyone found out about once I first shifted. They don't like me much."

Somehow, I can tell that she's putting it mildly. My expression turns stormy at the implications of how she must've grown up. No wonder she was wary of predators. And then we went and treated her like garbage. I wish I could kick my own ass. Penn and Lafe obviously have followed the same line of thought, because they go through varying degrees of pissed and contrite.

Penn recovers first. "Don't worry, Addie. We'll come up with a plan. We'll take care of them for you."

She smirks and pats him on the chest. "Boys, boys, boys," she says while clucking her tongue at us. "I don't need you to take care of them for me. I'm an Aberrant. We've dealt with our fair share of asshole pred packs. We already have a plan."

Her pluckiness and fight just makes me want her even more, and I can't help but be impressed. Most chicks would be ready to cower or have their mates take care of everything.

"What's the plan?" Lafe asks curiously.

"Sorry, it's a Pack Aberrant secret, and you aren't a misfit."

Lafe reaches forward and snags her by the waist, lifting her up onto the counter in one fluid motion and making her squeal in surprise. "Maybe ducks don't have the best hearing, but I'll say it again for you. We're your mates, and we aren't leaving. If you're a misfit, then so are we."

She smiles, her blue eyes lighting up her whole face. "I guess we should go talk to Alpha Hugo then. But I have to warn you, he won't take in just anybody."

Lafe grins and steps closer, so his hips meet the space between her thighs. "Liar."

"It's true," she insists, although I can tell that she's trying to keep a straight face. "I'm not sure you three are up to snuff. Aberrants have certain standards, you know."

"I'm sure we can prove ourselves."

She grins. "Good. Then let's go teach those Rockhead jerkoffs why you shouldn't mess with misfits."

15

PENN

Usually, when a shifter applies to join a new pack, you have to complete some sort of loyalty test first—like what Rockhead wants us to do by getting Addie. Other packs sometimes make applicants go up against some of their best fighters, and you can only earn a place in the pack if you win the fight.

Shifter laws and ways of life are a bit barbaric still, but it's what we've always known. We know loyalty through action, and we know strength through fights. So it surprises the hell out of me when Hugo looks over the three of us and tells us that all we have to do is have a meeting with him. I should've known that it wouldn't be as easy as it sounded.

We raced straight here from the pet shop and told him everything. After we filled him in, Hugo came up with a plan for how to handle Rockhead, but now, he's handling *us.* And it's pretty fucking terrifying.

"You formed a mate bond with one of *my* shifters," he says, standing tall and pissed off.

We're outside of his office, standing in the dirt between his Jeep and five of his enforcers, all dressed in their black fatigues. His second-in-command is glaring at us so thoroughly, that I'm surprised we haven't spontaneously combusted.

"We did," I answer him.

"You formed a quad, and then left my pack member to suffer. You abandoned her. Hurt her. Could have *killed her.*"

I wince and swallow hard. In my peripheral, I can see that Lafe has dropped his head in shame.

"We did," I say again. "We were wrong to judge her duck. We want to make it up to her—prove ourselves. And we would be honored if you'd let us join Pack Aberrant."

"Why should I let three fuckhead preds like you join *my* pack?" he snarls.

God, he's a scary motherfucker. Tall and bulky, with a scowl that could shatter glass. He's wearing torn jeans, a leather vest, and black boots that could probably break my ass in half if he decided to kick me. I really hope he doesn't kick me.

"You're right, we don't deserve to," Herrick speaks up. "But we realize our mistake. We were taught to believe that anything less than a perfect pred shifter was beneath us. We were wrong."

My eyes dart from Herrick back to Hugo. His scowl is still there. Dammit.

"Alpha, if you let us, we swear that we will prove ourselves to you. And to her," Lafe puts in.

"Why should I trust the word of a pred who didn't even have the respect to stay with his newly mated female?" Hugo demands.

"Hugo…" Addie begins, but he cuts her off with a single look.

"You go on now, Aderyn. I need to speak with these three alone," he tells her.

She cocks a brow. "Are you gonna be nice?" she asks.

"No."

She blinks at him and then shrugs, like—*what can you do?* —before wiggling her fingers at us. "Have fun. I'll go get ready to leave. You can meet me in the warehouse after."

She turns to leave, and right as we're all distracted, watching her walk off—okay, fine, we're watching her ass —Hugo shifts.

Having a huge, two-hundred-fifty pound albino jaguar suddenly in your face is a surefire way to piss your pants.

Lafe nearly trips on his own feet trying to back away, but we're all too slow to dodge the swipe that the alpha takes at us. All three of us land on our asses, dazed, and look up at his bared teeth and white fur. His spots are faded, and he has scars running down his torso, all the way to his swishing tail. Every inch of him is muscular, and his form radiates alpha power, making us realize just how strong he really is.

"Please don't maim us," Lafe tells him from his spot on the ground.

The alpha growls at him.

"Shut up, Lafe," Herrick snaps, making the alpha then turn and growl at *him*.

"Both of you shut up," I tell them, and yep, you guessed it, Hugo then growls at me.

He keeps on growling, letting his power wash over us, and I don't need shifter hearing to catch the melodic giggle coming from behind us. Yep. That's Addie laughing at us right now.

When I try to turn around to look at her, his massive paw comes out again and smacks me upside the head and *damn.* That has some kick to it. I have to shake my head to clear it, and the enforcers standing around smirk and chuckle at our expense.

When the jaguar gets in our faces and snarls some more, all three of us are forced into a shift. Our coyotes come out, immediately bowing in respect to the powerful alpha. The jaguar paces in front of the three of us where we're crouched on the ground, and when he bites down on my neck, my coyote knows better than to struggle.

This is a pivotal moment for any shifter wanting to join a new pack. Our animals know their place, and they sense Hugo's power and immediately defer to him. What would be worrying is if our coyotes *didn't* submit. That would mean our animals didn't recognize him as an alpha, and we wouldn't be able to join his pack.

When Hugo has drawn a little blood on all three of our necks, he roars again, but then swipes his tongue over the marks, and I sigh in relief. By doing that, it means he's accepted his role as our alpha—he's accepted us into his pack. Which is pretty fucking surprising, considering I was pretty sure he was about to toss us out on our asses. Hell, we deserve it.

But for some reason, he didn't. I can already feel the new alpha bond taking over, like a buzz through my skin, and a settled feeling gathers deep in my gut. For shifters, being rogue is not our preferred state. Our animals naturally want to join packs and live together.

I'd forgotten what it felt like to have that alpha-pack bond. Now, it feels like everything has clicked into place inside of my spirit. I belong to a pack again, I have a mate, and everything is connecting together and giving me a sense of belonging and peace.

Hugo roars one last time before shifting back. My coyote looks up at him, and when Hugo walks forward, holding his fingers out to me, my coyote sniffs him tentatively. When he's done getting his scent signature, he licks Hugo's fingertips. The alpha pats my coyote's head, and then moves down the line, doing the same thing to Lafe and Herrick.

When he's done, Hugo looks down at us. "Shift."

Our coyotes instantly retreat, and we stand up again, yanking on our dusty jeans and shirts. I swipe at the puncture on my neck from where he bit me, but it's already healing.

"Come on," Hugo says to us, one of his enforcers passing him some new clothes. His didn't survive his shift, considering how fucking big his jaguar is.

Hugo turns to walk to his Jeep, and the three of us exchange a look before climbing in. I take the front seat while Lafe and Herrick settle in the back. He has the top off, so there's just bars and wind around us as Hugo starts driving. With one hand on the steering wheel, he takes a right and points to a modest-sized house with a long drive and overgrown grass. "That's my place. Back that way are the mate cabins. Over there are the singles' warehouses. The rec center and our own gym is this way. We train there. Training is mandatory for every shifter in the pack."

"Even the females?" Lafe asks, surprised.

I have the same reaction, because it's rare that females are allowed to train and fight. Usually, they're kept as the caretakers. It's medieval and stupid, but most shifters are stuck in the old ways.

"*Especially* the females," Hugo answers. "Most of my pack members don't have predator animals that can protect them in a fight. So we train their human forms to be able to defend themselves, and then we train their prey animal forms to use their own unique strengths to their advantages."

"Smart," Herrick says.

Hugo turns down a dirt road and looks at Herrick in the rearview mirror. "Pack Aberrant has to be smart. We don't have brute strength. Our power comes from something else."

"What's that?"

"You'll have to figure that out on your own."

Hugo parks his Jeep in front of the rec center, where a dozen or so shifters are hanging around. Next to the metal building, there's an outdoor eating area, set up with dozens of picnic tables and a pile of wood for a bonfire. On the other side is a training yard, enclosed in a short wooden fence. There are two enforcers overlooking a training session going on between four shifters—two females and two males, all in their human form.

When some of the bystanders notice Hugo, they wave and smile and he tilts his head at them in greeting. "Alpha," a female says, coming up to the side of the Jeep. She's wearing loose sweats on her body and a toddler on her hip.

"Hey, Janie. How's it looking today?" he asks her.

Janie casts her eyes over at the training yard where the shifters are running through moves, with shouted orders and direction coming from the enforcers. I can see immediately how well they're all working together. The sense of camaraderie is strong, and when one of the training females manages to pin the male she's fighting onto the ground, everyone cheers for her—even the male she beat.

Janie smiles. "It's going real well, Alpha."

"Good. And how are you, kid?"

The toddler takes the thumb out of his mouth and beams. "I'm two!"

Hugo chuckles at the two drool-covered fingers the boy is holding up proudly. He musses his hair. "You mind your mother, alright?"

The little boy nods. "Okay."

Janie smiles and nods at us before walking away, heading back toward the fence line. I watch as the little boy hops off her hip and starts chasing a cricket that's jumping around on the grass.

Hugo nods at her back. "Janie joined Pack Aberrant eight years ago. Showed up bloody and near unconscious at our gate," he explains, his voice low but steady. "She'd been beaten within an inch of her life, all because her family of cottontails lived next to the territory of a pack of wolves. The wolf shifters ambushed them in their den one night, for no reason other than the fact that they could. They killed every last one of them. A dozen lives lost in a single night, just like that," he says, snapping his fingers.

"Janie only managed to escape because her rabbit was fast. She lost her parents, her aunts and uncles, her cousins and siblings...everyone. The alpha wolf shifter beat her, and then used his power to force her to shift into her rabbit form. They thought it was entertaining sport to make the terrified and injured rabbits run from his wolves, and then watch them be caught and mauled to death. Janie got away, though. She ran and she didn't stop running until she'd crossed two states to find Pack Aberrant. It took three years for me to convince her to shift into her rabbit form again. Another year to get that haunted look out of her eye. And still to this day, she's terrified of a wolf's howl."

Fuck. I have to swallow down the bile that's pushing up my throat.

"She mated three years ago to another pack member," Hugo goes on, and we follow his gaze to one of the enforcers in the ring. I instantly see the resemblance of his bright blond hair to that of the little boy still running around, now with dirt and a smile smeared across his face.

"Collins is blind," Hugo says, making my eyes widen in surprise. "His pack of cougar shifters exiled him for it as soon as he was of age. He lived rogue for five years before he heard about this pack and asked to join. He's a damn good fighter, despite his lack of sight, and he sees what other people don't. He's observant; he can tell what people are doing wrong by listening to the way their bodies sound when they move, and he inspires some of our physically weaker shifters by showing them that they can be strong."

I watch as the enforcer turns his head, as if listening, and then whirls around and snatches Janie's hand from where she was trying to creep up on him on the other side of the fence. She tips her head back and laughs, and the enforcer claims her mouth with a kiss.

Hugo turns to look at all of us. "Each and every one of my pack members has a story like that, Addie included. She was born into Pack Rockhead—a pred-only pack, and they punished her for it everyday of her life for fifteen years until she was exiled."

My hands curl into fists. The fact that my mate was forced to grow up like that makes fury coalesce in my veins.

"I found her at a gas station. She was skin and bones, with hollow eyes and fear evaporating off of her skin. I love her like a daughter," he tells us sternly, looking each one of us in the eye. "She's a duck. A prey bird that the rest of the shifter world will look down on. Hell, even other Canes will look down on her. But she's loyal, and kind, and smart—and if you fucking hurt her, I will fucking hurt you *worse*."

I know he's serious. I can feel it in the alpha bond. If we hurt Addie, there will be a reckoning.

I know that Alpha Hugo isn't just powerful or strong. In the short amount of time I've known him, I've also learned what a *good* male he is. He takes in shifters who are different, and he gives them a place to belong. He makes the weak have strength. He makes the prey learn that they don't have to run. He gives the misfits a place to fit.

I don't know why the hell he's decided to accept us into his pack, but I'm so fucking honored that I can't speak. I can feel how different this pack is. It's a family.

I'll never be half the shifter that Janie or Collins is. Hell, I'll never be as strong as Addie had to be when she was just a girl. These shifters have been through hell— shunned and beaten, bullied and *hated*, all because they weren't born as the perfect preds that our society demands.

Shame washes over me for ever sharing those kinds of hateful prejudices, and because I know my best friends better than I know myself, I know that Herrick and Lafe are feeling the same exact things that I am. Heavy emotion burns the back of my throat, and my Adam's apple bobs up and down.

"We understand now," Lafe says quietly. And he's right. We do.

Hugo studies him for a long moment, and then looks over Herrick and me. I feel like he's looking into my fucking *soul* as he watches me, and as my alpha, I submit to him. I want to be a part of this pack. I want to help protect these shifters. I want to earn my place as a member of Pack Aberrant, and be the mate that Addie deserves.

After what feels like an eternity has passed, Hugo finally nods. "Good," he says to us, like he sees the huge impact he just made in us. He holds out his hand for me to shake. "Welcome to Pack Aberrant."

My coyote howls inside of me. Lafe is grinning, and Herrick dips his head in thanks.

This—this right here. This is why we left our old pack. We weren't exactly sure what we were looking for, but we actually found it. And we sure as hell aren't going to let shitty, hateful shifters like Rockhead mess with our new pack or our mate. They'll have to go through us first.

16

ADDIE

"Sneaking away?"

Jetta tenses and stops in her tracks at my voice. She turns around, finding me up in the warehouse catwalk on the second floor. I came back to my place to shower and get ready for tonight, while the guys stayed back with Hugo for their pack initiation meeting. Hopefully it's going well. I left right after Hugo shifted into his jaguar form and swiped a clawed paw at all three of the guys, making them land on their asses.

Hugo roared at them a little too, no doubt telling them off for how they treated me. Gotta say, it filled me with the warm and fuzzies. If that isn't fatherly love, I don't know what is.

I take the stairs down to meet Jetta, who has a plastic grocery bag slung over her arm. She's wearing the same outfit as the day she came here, tattered jean shorts with black fishnets, and her signature leather jacket. Her black and white hair is pulled back into a tight ponytail, and other than the deep red lipstick, her face is bare.

My eyes flick down to the bag in her hand. "If you were gonna run away, you could've at least stolen more clothes."

She snorts. "Your clothes are a bit too preppy and nerdy for me. How is it you have a drawer full of *Napoleon Dynamite* shirts right next to girly ass frilly skirts, but you don't own a single plain black t-shirt?"

"My taste is sophisticated."

She smiles without showing any teeth, and I lean against the doorway. "You could stay, you know."

She sighs and swipes a hand across her perfectly arched brows. "I know. But the troupe master will be after me, and I don't want your pack to suffer because of me."

"We can handle him."

"I appreciate the confidence, but I know him and what he's capable of. You don't want that here."

"What I don't want is for you to leave."

"Addie…"

"Come on, Jetta. Talk to Hugo. You can trust him. If you give him more information, we can try to stay one step ahead of your old troupe master. But he can't track you," I remind her, looking down at the collar that's still wrapped around her pale neck. "And he doesn't know you're here. I'm not saying you have to join Pack Aberrant right this second, but you should think about it at least. These shifters...they're my family. You deserve to have that too. They'll accept you exactly as you are, and we can help you with Troupe Delirium."

"I don't need you all to fight my battles."

"I know that. I've seen you fight, remember?"

She looks at the door and shuffles on her feet. I can see the indecision warring in her eyes. She *wants* to stay. She just needs to know that she's wanted. I don't think Jetta has ever been wanted before. Owned, yes. Expected to perform, definitely. But wanted and accepted for who she is? Never.

"Maybe you don't have to do things on your own anymore," I tell her. "No one is beating down our gates. Stay. Get to know everyone. Talk to Hugo. Then, if you still want to leave, I'll personally make sure you have black t-shirts to steal before you go."

She laughs lightly and chews on her lip. I want so badly for her to stay, but I know that I can't push her. She's never been free before. She's been kept in a collar all her life. She should be able to decide how to live, and if she chooses to walk, then I'll support her.

"Dammit, Aderyn Locke," she finally sighs. "Why'd you have to go and convince me?"

I beam and reach for her bag before she can change her mind. "Really? You'll stay?"

She hands it over and nods. "For now."

"It's a deal," I say, ecstatic.

"What's a deal?"

I turn to see all three of my coyote mates strutting inside from the back door. "Jetta is staying on pack land for a while," I say happily. "How about you three? How did it go with Hugo?" I'm trying not to be nervous, but...I'm nervous. Hugo is protective of me, and he's an excellent judge of character. What if he denied them? What will I do?

But my fear is instantly alleviated when Lafe turns his neck and I see a leftover smear of blood and a healing mark. "You're in the pack?" I ask hopefully.

A grin spreads over his face. "We're in the pack."

Giddy, I jump up and down before flinging my arms around all three of them, smooshing them together. One of them presses his lips to my temple. Another one squeezes my ass.

Jetta puts a hand on her cocked hip and eyes them, glaring until we pull apart. "So. You're the three asshole coyotes who mated with my girl here."

"That's us," Lafe says, chipper as can be.

In a move that I would've missed if I'd blinked, Jetta suddenly shifts her weight, and jabs Penn in the gut. Breath escapes him with an "oof" as he hunches over, but Jetta is already away, doing this super impressive spinny move that catches Herrick in the throat with the edge of her palm. He curses as he hacks, and then she leaps in front of Lafe. He flings up his arms in front of him. "Uncle! I fuckin' surrender!"

Jetta stops short with an unimpressed snort. She looks over at me, eyebrow cocked. "This is your trio of mates?"

I laugh at Penn who's still trying to stand upright, and at Herrick who continues to cough. Lafe is pretending that he didn't just edge behind me, but...he totally did and I'm currently shielding him from Jetta's attacks.

"Yep. Aren't they great?" I beam.

Jetta rolls her eyes and takes her bag back from my hands. "If I'm staying, I want in on the Pack Rockhead retaliation," she says as she starts to stalk away. The guys watch her warily as her combat boots clank up the metal steps.

"Okie dokie! I'll let Hugo know."

She gives me a wave before disappearing into her room. I look back at the guys, barely able to contain my mirth. "You guys are so tough."

"She came at me out of nowhere," Penn grumbles.

"That female is ducking scary," Lafe says, finally coming out from behind me. "What kind of shifter is she?"

I shake my head. "First rule of Pack Aberrant, we don't divulge each other's animals. They'll let you know what they shift into once they like you."

"Pretty sure that one doesn't like us," Herrick says dryly.

I shrug. "We were each other's first friends, and you were a jerk to me."

He tilts his head side to side. "Fair enough."

Lafe eyes the spot Jetta had been. "I bet she's a honey badger or some shit. Those things are vicious."

I just laugh. "Does Hugo want us to get ready to go?" I ask.

Penn nods. "Yep. He asked us to come get you. We're leaving in ten." I nod, steeling myself for tonight. Penn notices and his eyes soften. "Hey, you okay? If you don't want to be the bait, just say the word and we'll talk to Hugo. You don't have to do this if you don't want to."

"No, I want to," I reply with determination. "I want to help take Rockhead down a notch."

Jetta suddenly pops up out of nowhere behind us. "Me too, let's go."

Lafe flinches. "Dammit, female!" he exclaims. "You're like a freaking ninja."

She chuckles at him as she yanks open the front door. "Come on, preds. I'll protect you."

I pat Lafe on the shoulder as they grumble about how tough they are, and follow Jetta outside. "You *sure* they're coyotes?" she asks me, making me laugh.

"I'm sure. Lafe accidentally shifted when he saw me in the shower earlier."

She snorts. "Males."

I cast a look over my shoulder, catching all three of them staring at my ass. I smile and face forward again. Yep, males. And they're *mine.*

17
PENN

I look around at the other twenty or so members from Pack Rockhead as we stand in the wooded area behind the parking lot of *Joystick*, the gamer club that Addie and her friends are positioned in.

Herrick and Lafe have already shifted, as have about half of Rockhead's shifters, but I'm still in my human form. I eye the wolves and bobcats warily, worrying that our plan is somehow going to fall apart.

If Addie gets hurt, or any of her—*our*—pack gets hurt either...No. I can't think like that right now. All I can do is trust that Alpha Hugo knows what he's doing, and do what I'm told.

If we want to be new enforcers for the pack, we have to show that we're dependable and can follow orders. We already royally fucked up with Addie, so if we have any hope of earning Hugo's respect, we have to prove ourselves worthy of her *and* Pack Aberrant.

After Drag texted me the whereabouts of Addie, he ordered us to follow her. So we did. Right back to Pack Aberrant land where we told Alpha Hugo everything, of course. He came up with the plan, and with his direction, we acted as informants to Rockhead, letting them know that Addie and some of her other packmates had come here for the night.

Drag ordered us to wait here while he brought reinforcements in. He'd been practically giddy over the phone when I called to tell him we'd tracked her and a dozen of her packmates here. He'd been thrilled at the thought that he'd be able to take more of them down to teach Addie a lesson.

Fucker.

Their plan is to not only take Addie, but to also rough up the rest of her pack members in the process. Herrick, Lafe, and I have had to deal with listening to what they plan to do to Addie for the past hour. At one point, I had to physically hold Herrick back while Lafe distracted them.

Drag is talking with the last group of Rockhead shifters that just showed up about five minutes ago. One of them is a bear shifter named Jordy. He's a spindly fuckhead, so unlike his animal, with thin, bony limbs and a weasel-looking face. I dislike him right away, but it really seals the deal when he starts joking with Drag about how Addie deserves everything coming to her.

"Hey, you must be the newbies," Jordy says, sidling up beside me. Herrick and Lafe's coyotes step closer with a low growl. Jordy looks at them with amusement. "Coyotes, huh? Don't have many of those in our pack."

"Hmm."

"I hear you're gonna be a Rockie after this. But you all were in the Moon Pack, so you'll fit right in. We're a strong pred pack. You're about to see a dose of that tonight when we put these weak little freaks in their place."

It takes all my self-control to keep from cocking a fist and throwing it into his face.

He's looking at me expectantly, like he's just waiting for me to laugh with him at Pack Aberrant's expense. And if I don't want to blow my cover, that's what I should do. But I can't bring myself to do it. When I keep silent, he opens his mouth to say more, but before he can, Lafe lifts his leg and pisses all over Jordy's boot.

He recoils and moves to kick at Lafe's coyote, but Lafe dodges him. "What the fuck? Gross, man!"

"Huh. Guess he doesn't like you much."

Jordy grimaces at his piss soaked pant leg and shoots the animal a glare. "Fucking coyotes," he mutters before stalking away.

I look down at Lafe with a smirk. "Real subtle, dude."

The coyote's tongue lolls out of his mouth happily.

"Alright, listen up," Drag announces, making everyone stop and pay attention to him. "I just got the message from Riot. Looks like they're about to leave, so everyone get in your positions. Let's fuck them up and remind them why they don't mess with Pack Rockhead," he says, excitement thick in his words. Several of the other shifters whoop and clap at his words. "The girl is mine to take. Everyone else, it's a free for all," he says with a vicious grin.

Malicious anticipation ripples over the group, and several of the shifted pack members start pacing and growling. Herrick's coyote snaps at some of them as they go by. He might be smaller than the wolves, but he's a force to be reckoned with. I once saw him take down a buffalo all on his own.

Drag comes stalking over to stand in front of me. "Good job boys," he tells us. "You led us right to her. Alpha Rourn is pleased. He might even let you watch Aderyn's punishment later."

I clench my fists at my sides and my eye ticks with fury that I try to contain beneath my skin.

When his phone vibrates again, he looks down at it with a grin. "They're comin' now."

Drag just thinks those text messages are from his man, Riot. But really, he's been texting someone from Aberrant all night. The misfits might not be the strongest physically, but they're resourceful and smart. They know how to hack, plan, and play to their strengths.

"Get ready," I mutter to Herrick and Lafe. They both pull up on their haunches, getting ready to spring into action.

I keep my eyes trained on the gamer club across the

parking lot with the rest of Rockhead, and within seconds, the door to Joystick opens, and Addie and ten more of her pack members come piling out.

Drag whistles low, and we all take off at a run. The plan is to sneak up behind the "unsuspecting" misfits and attack them, while Drag takes Addie. Not that we'd let that fucking happen.

Herrick and Lafe race ahead of me, heading straight for Addie.

Drag notices and growls. "Hey! I said she's mine!"

I ignore him as I pump my legs faster, trying to reach Addie's group before Pack Rockhead does. No fucking way are we letting a single shifter touch her.

Her group is walking together through the otherwise empty parking lot, seeming completely oblivious to the ambush running up behind them. Herrick and Lafe's feet hit the pavement first, but the other Rockhead wolves are hot on their heels.

I force myself to run faster, and right before the oncoming Rockhead shifters reach Addie and her group, she and the others drop the unsuspecting act and turn around to face them. This takes Rockhead by surprise, and several of their steps falter, but with an order from Drag, they keep going.

Jordy, all skin and bones in his human form is a fast fucker, and nearly beats us to reach Addie. Addie braces herself, but Herrick leaps onto Jordy's back at the last second, his teeth digging into Jordy's side, sending him to the ground.

As soon as he's flat on his back, the rest of Rockhead is here, and the two packs clash together. Fights break out as several of the Aberrants move to the forefront, protecting their other packmates. Hugo purposely chose some of his enforcers to be present, since they're the ones best trained to fight.

I finally reach Addie, with Lafe flanking her other side. She smiles at me. "Right on time."

Hearing a snarl, we look back to see Jordy smacking off Herrick's coyote with a powerful kick to the belly. Herrick is dislodged and thrown off, and Jordy has menace in his eyes as he gets to his feet. Herrick curls his spine and bares his teeth, ready to meet Jordy with his own attack, but Jetta suddenly appears out of nowhere. She assaults him with a barrage of lightning-fast movements—a strike to his stomach, a kick to the back of the knees, and well placed temple hit, and he's out like a light.

She looks down at him like she's disappointed it didn't last longer and then shoots Herrick a cocky smirk. "Told you I'd protect you preds." Herrick yips and she bounds away, light on her feet, off to go help some of the other Aberrants. Now I'm really fucking curious as to what her animal is.

The members of Pack Rockhead are mostly big, muscled, arrogant shifters; whereas Aberrant look more like a bunch of nerds. But underneath their graphic tees and glasses, the misfits are surprisingly capable, and they take several Rockheads off guard. Still, we're outnumbered, and Hugo didn't want to send all obvious fighters with Addie, in case Rockhead got tipped off, so some of them are barely holding their own. I look around for our back up, but they aren't here yet.

"Get the girl!"

Drag's voice cuts through all the noises of fists punching, people grunting, and shifters growling and snapping their teeth.

He's pointing at her, looking at me expectantly as he levels a misfit with a fist to the jaw. I grab Addie and yank her behind me. Herrick and Lafe flank me, so that we're standing as a united front when he comes stalking forward.

"You fucking double-crossers!" he yells, his skin mottling red with his rage. "You're preds! What the fuck are you doing protecting a shifter like *her?*"

"She's our mate, and she's ten times the shifter you are."

He rears a fist back and aims it for me, but I crouch down and then launch myself at him, catching him in the stomach with my shoulder. We both go down hard onto the pavement, in a whirl of fists and feet, and my skin starts rippling with fur, my animal desperate to come out and attack the male who's threatening our mate.

Drag uses his massive body size to toss me off, and my head slams against the pavement. Before he can get to his feet, Herrick and Lafe are there, biting his wrists and ankles to keep him down.

"Addie!"

My head whips around at her friend Zoey's voice, and when I turn, I see that fucking sleazebag Jordy dragging Addie away. He's got a knife to her neck and his fist around her hair. And I lose my shit.

I roar and my animal bursts out of me with uncontrollable rage. My coyote is pissed and out for blood, especially when he sees Addie wincing from Jordy's hold on her.

Herrick and Lafe are still dealing with Drag, but my coyote is strong, and his protective instincts make him even more fierce. A vicious howl tears from my coyote's throat, and Addie's eyes lock with me. One second, she's struggling against Jordy as he pulls her toward a waiting SUV, and the next, her duck bursts out of her.

Jordy immediately loses his hold, and all I see are a flurry of tawny feathers and a snapping beak. Her duck latches onto Jordy's pointy nose, and the guy starts screeching in pain as he tries to dash her away. Too bad for him, he doesn't notice that her friend Zoey has also shifted into her snake, and has managed to wrap herself around his leg. With a warning hiss (and a rattler with no rattle,) the snake sinks its fangs into his calf.

Jordy's screech turns into a scream, and Zoey's snake quickly disengages and slithers away before he can try to yank on her. Addie's duck still has a good hold on his nose, and all his crazed flailing makes him go falling back. The second he lands, he shifts into his bear form with a roar, bursting out of his clothes, and Addie's duck is forced to let go.

Before his massive brown paw can take a swipe at her, my coyote's jaw is locked around his neck. He's still on his back on the pavement, so his bear desperately tries to throw me off, but my coyote wants blood. He digs his teeth in more, showing the bear exactly who has the upper hand.

"Penn."

My coyote hears her voice, but it doesn't register. Blood flows into his mouth, the bear's throat locked inside. All it will take is one tug—one jerk of his head, and my coyote will rip his throat out.

"Penn. Stop."

My coyote's eyes flare wide at our mate when she steps in his line of vision. She crouches in front of him. "You can let go. He's not worth it."

My coyote whines low, craving more of the bear's blood, wanting to sink his teeth in deeper, punish him for hurting our mate. But Addie gently brings a hand up and brushes it against my coyote's side. "Come on, Penn. Come back."

My coyote watches her clear blue eyes and he senses her distress. Finally, my coyote's jaw unlocks, and he steps away from the bear. As soon as he retreats the slightest bit, I take over and shove myself back into the forefront. I shift back, and look around, seeing that our reinforcements have finally showed up.

Drag is standing now with a couple of his packmates, staring down Herrick and Lafe. He's bleeding in several places and looks like he wants to rip apart their coyotes, but he's outnumbered now, and he knows it.

I look back down at Jordy at my feet. In my human form, I'm able to study Jordy's bear more thoroughly, and I realize he's worse off than I'd originally thought. His throat is bleeding slightly, but not with a killing puncture, but his leg where Zoey's snake bit him has swelled up at least twice the size.

It appears that he's gone unconscious too, whether from the venom or hitting his head on the pavement, I'm not sure. Still, I'm struggling keeping myself together. This male hurt my mate, and all of my instincts are screaming at me to end him.

Like she can sense my struggle, Addie comes forward and takes my hand, squeezing it reassuringly. The other members of Pack Aberrant have surrounded the entire parking lot, but Pack Rockhead is still fighting viciously, despite being suddenly outnumbered.

When I see Drag and two other males trying to take a cheap shot from behind at Jetta, I nearly shift again, but a booming voice cuts through the parking lot and makes every shifter in the vicinity immediately freeze. "Enough!"

Even the Pack Rockhead shifters stop and turn to Alpha Hugo. They can't help it. When an alpha of his power uses a particular tone, the magic in us responds to his natural authority.

Hugo steps forward, from the fifty or so members of Pack

Aberrant that are surrounding the parking lot. Drag and the other members of Rockhead eye them nervously.

Hugo's second-in-command, a huge motherfucker with tattoos on his neck, is holding up a tablet. Even from a distance, I can see the entire scene is being transmitted to a man with slicked back brown hair and a scar down his cheek.

"Alpha Rourn," Addie mutters beside me as she presses closer, which makes me realize that like many others who shifted back, we're both stark naked.

"As you can see," Hugo drawls, his voice carrying across the lot. "It looks like your shifters have breached our peace treaty, Rourn. They've crossed into Pack Aberrant territory without permission and attacked my pack members, unprovoked."

Hugo's second-in-command shifts the tablet, allowing the other shifter man to see the mess of broken up fights and injured shifters all over the lot.

"Yes. I see that," he says with a clipped tone.

Rockhead's alpha is clearly pissed, but he's not pissed because his shifters are attacking. No, he knew damn well they were. Hell, he sanctioned it. But he can't admit that unless he wants a full-blown pack war, which he doesn't.

Hugo is a damn smart alpha, which means he knows his enemies and how they operate. Alpha Rourn is trying to punish Addie and weaken the Aberrants, but sends small groups to do the jobs, while keeping up fake appearances of an alliance.

He had no intention of acting with honor. He's hiring humans to do his dirty work, like robbing banks, and he's doing all of this in order to appear honest and law abiding, while secretly working to rule the entire town. He wants to pretend that his pack members are acting out of order so he can avoid the repercussions. And there would be repercussions, because the leader of *all* the shifter packs in the continental U.S.—Alpha Leader Lutzo, *also* happens to be connected on the video call.

Hugo knew that Rockhead's M.O. was to fight under-handed and dirty. Which is why he planned this to go down this way. We needed proof showing Rockhead shifters attacking Aberrants, which we have, and Alpha Leader Lutzo doesn't look happy *at all.*

"What's the meaning of this, Rockhead Alpha? Are you declaring war on Pack Aberrant?"

"No, sir," Alpha Rourn grits out through clenched teeth.

"So these Rockhead shifters acted out of orders?" Alpha Leader Lutzo questions with a cock of his brow.

"It would appear so."

Lutzo's eyes blaze through the screen. I can almost feel his alpha power just from video alone, which is impossible. But he's a massive crocodile, with so much alpha power that he was a shoe-in for the job. Shifters need someone strong to lead them, especially in order to lead other alphas, but Lutzo fits the bill.

"Tell me, Alpha Rourn, are you incapable of leading your own pack?" Lutzo asks, his tone even but sharp. "Because if that is the case, I will dissolve you as Rockhead Alpha, and assign someone who *can* do the job and lead these shifters properly."

"That won't be necessary," Rourn says indignantly.

"Then I suggest you control your shifters. Or I'll do it for you." The warning is thick in the air, and the other members of Rockhead shuffle nervously on their feet. The last thing they would want is for a new leader come in, or for their pack to be dissolved.

Alpha Rourn grits his teeth, twin spots of red appearing high on his cheeks. "Rockhead," he bellows out. "Stand down and get your asses back to our pack land. Now." Without another word, he disconnects the call, leaving only Alpha Leader Lutzo on the screen.

"Alpha Hugo, it is within your rights to declare war on Pack Rockhead for their attack. What is your decision?"

The Rockhead's anxiety seems to spike as Hugo takes his time sweeping a level look over them. He lets them bask in their nervousness for a moment. "We are a peaceful pack. If Rockhead agrees to honor their peace treaty, Pack Aberrant will forgive them once for their transgression."

"A merciful decision," Lutzo says with a nod. "Very well. I suggest you monitor this situation. Notify me if another unsanctioned attack occurs," he finishes.

"I will," Hugo agrees, and the video call ends.

His second hands off the tablet to another shifter, and then crosses his arms to glare at Rockhead while Hugo does the same. "You heard your alpha. Unless you're going to throw a formal challenge right here, right now *without* the approval of your alpha, then get off my land," he thunders. "I'm being lenient this time, but if another Rockhead shifter attacks one of my packmates, I won't be so lenient anymore. I'll declare war on your pack and have the backing of Alpha Leader Lutzo. I'm sure that's not the kind of attention your pack wants. The council might be tempted to look into your *other* activities." Hugo gives Drag a pointed look, and the rest of the Rockhead shifters defer to him, tense and awaiting his orders.

Drag stares Hugo down and spits at his feet. "We'll get off *your land*," Drag sneers. His eyes dart over to Jetta, who's standing off to the side. "Funny that," he says with a tilt of his head. "If I didn't know any better, I'd say that was a collar."

Jetta tenses, but Hugo's face gives nothing away. Addie's hand squeezes mine tightly.

Drag studies Jetta from head to toe in a slow perusal. She doesn't cower at all, just stands tall and meets him eye for eye.

"In fact, I seem to remember collars that looked just like that," Drag says ominously. "I think I'll give Troupe Delirium a call. I'm suddenly in the mood for some...*entertainment.*"

Jetta moves to launch herself at him, but one of the Aberrant enforcers hooks his arms under hers and manages to hold her back. Drag grins darkly. "That's what I thought."

Turning his head, he whistles, and he and the rest of Pack Rockhead start walking away. A couple of them scoop up a still unconscious Jordy, and a growl escapes my throat. All of us stay still and rigid, tension high in the air. It isn't until they get in their cars and drive away that everyone seems to take a collective breath.

The enforcer finally lets Jetta go, and she thanks him with a glare and an elbow to the gut, making him curl over with an *"oomph."* Poor fucker.

Drag is gonna be a problem. Especially for Jetta. But we have time, and now that I've seen Hugo operate, I have every confidence that he can prepare for what's to come.

Hugo looks around at his pack. "Everyone alright?"

"Hell, yeah! We owned those Rockhead assholes!" Zoey shouts back at him. She looks over at me. "No offense."

I chuckle. "None taken. Nice bite by the way."

"Thank you," she beams.

"Alpha Hugo, what took you so long to get here?" I ask, trying real fucking hard not to sound like an insolent little prick.

"Rockhead scouts," Hugo answers. "We had to backtrack, otherwise they would've tipped the others off that we were coming to ambush them."

"How much did Alpha Leader Lutzo see?" another shifter asks.

"Enough," Hugo answers simply. "Now let's all get back to the compound. Good work, everyone."

The pack begins to disperse, some of the enforcers

helping up the others who were injured during the fights. Herrick and Lafe have shifted back into their human forms already and are pulling on clothes from where we stashed them earlier behind one of the cars.

They toss me some clothes too, and then Herrick comes stalking toward Addie with a frown on his face. He picks up the clothes that she'd shed when she shifted, and carefully pulls her shirt over her head.

He lifts her hair out in a tender gesture and then hands over her pants. "There, mate."

Her eyes soften at his reverent and protective tone, and she pulls on her pants and then plants a kiss on his cheek. "Thanks."

I quickly get dressed, noticing that other shifters are doing the same, while some choose to stay in their animal forms. And it *is* a motley crew. Unlike most packs which are primarily three or four of the same kinds of animal, the misfits have no two alike. Just in my quick perusal, I see a moose with one antler, a mean ass looking boar, a koala, a swan, and...is that a poisonous toad?

Once Addie is settled and the three of us are surrounding her, she stops short and raises a brow at Lafe's new shirt. It's a white tee with the letters, *WTD* splayed across the chest.

"Really?" she says dryly. "WTD?"

Lafe grins and looks down at it proudly. "Yep. WTD is officially our new mate-pack slogan."

She shakes her head. "Nope."

"What the duck? Why not?" he demands.

She rolls her eyes and looks over at me. "You let him get shirts printed?"

I grin. "I'm pretty sure he got one in every color."

Lafe nods enthusiastically. "Yep. I got some that say, *Ducking Hell, Quack Addict,* and *Duck Off,* too. Oh, and I also got one for you that says, *I am se-duck-tive."*

Addie can't hold back her laugh anymore. She lets loose, and the sound bounces around, wrapping around the four of us. I fucking love that sound. I love her smile, too, and the way it makes her eyes crinkle at the corners. Clearly, Lafe and Herrick love it too, based on the way they're looking at her affectionately.

"I guess that'll go with the new pajama pants I got that say, *My Mates Are Howl-arious,"* she quips.

Lafe grins at her with punny pride.

Hugo walks up to us just then, interrupting our little powwow. "Good work. You three preds weren't completely useless," he says dryly by way of greeting. "You managed to get Rockhead right where we wanted them."

"Glad we could help," I say with a nod.

Just then, a tiny gerbil comes racing over to stand next to Hugo. In an instant, he shifts, turning back into the huge motherfucker—Hugo's second-in-command.

Lafe splutters. "You're a—a…gerbil?"

We can't help it. All three of us start chuckling.

But the shifter is not amused. He points a meaty finger in Lafe's face. "Keep laughing, and I'll shift, crawl up your asshole, and rip out your intestines."

Our laughs choke off. Lafe visibly pales. "Okay. Yep. Understood. No laughing."

Hugo looks amused, and he claps his Second on the back. "Oh, I forgot to tell you three. Now that you've joined our pack and want to become enforcers, Igor here is your new trainer."

I inwardly groan while Lafe curses under his breath. Gerbil Igor smiles a bit sadistically. "Tomorrow morning. Four A.M. sharp. Your coyote asses are mine."

"Oh. Umm. Awesome," I say.

With that, Hugo and Igor stroll away, and it's just us and Addie left in the parking lot. The rest of Aberrant have already left. I notice the huge smile spread across Addie's face as she tries to stifle her giggles. I take her by the elbow and start leading her to our car. "Oh, you think that's funny, do you?"

"Yep," she says with a bounce.

"Our mate wants to see us suffer?" Lafe asks.

"It'll be good for you," she says, patting him on the back. "Knock your cockiness down a peg or two."

I lean over and nip at her ear. "I love it when you say *cock*."

She snorts out a laugh as we get to the car.

When we all pile in, I breathe in, because no matter how

many times we've driven with the windows down, the smell of our activities from that first night of her heat-wave is still saturated in the upholstery. Lafe takes an exaggerated deep breath. "Ahh. That new sex smell."

Addie elbows him, but he just catches her arm and laughs. "Such a feisty thing," he says, tsking. "Hey, Herrick, which bird spends all their time on their knees?"

Herrick chuckles. "I don't know, which one?"

"Bird of prey."

"Or Addie," Herrick gibes.

"Hey!" Addie says, smacking him playfully on the arm. "You'll have to earn that sexual act."

Herrick grins wolfishly—or coyotishly? Whatever.

"Okay, I got a better one. And it's fitting, considering Addie was robbed," Lafe says with a grin. "What do you call a bird that steals?"

"What?"

"A robber ducky."

I chuckle as I watch her from the rearview mirror. Addie laughs and lightly hits him on the chest. "Are you ever gonna stop with the bird puns?"

Lafe pulls her leg over his thigh and starts kneading her skin. "Nope."

"You're a dweeb."

That makes Herrick laugh. "A dweeb? Who says that?"

"She likes to say okie dokie, too," I reply with a smirk.

"I'm eloquent and shit."

She's also aroused as hell. I can smell it.

"Say cock again," Lafe tells her, leaning in to trace his nose against her neck.

She shakes her head. "Nope. From now on, I'm going to call it anything *but* that."

I love it when she's feisty. "Oh, yeah? Like what?" Lafe asks.

"I'm with Lafe. Say cock. Or dick," I plead. I love to hear those filthy words coming out of her pretty little mouth.

"Nope," she says, barely containing a smile. "I'm going to call them jizzicles from now on. Or skin flutes. Or no, wait!" she says excitedly. "Quiver bones. Quiver bones all the way. That sounds like a winner."

"It sounds like something a drunk cupid would say," Herrick retorts.

She shrugs.

"I don't care what you call it, as long as I can bury it in your sweet cunt," Lafe says, pressing a kiss to the spot beneath her ear and tugging her hair to the side for better access.

"Don't start shit in here," I warn him. I had to drive during her heatwave and I don't need a repeat performance of that right now. It's torture having them go at it while I'm stuck in the driver's seat. I should start making one of these other assholes drive once and awhile so that I can have my way with her.

Luckily, it doesn't take us long to get back to the Aberrant compound. Hugo gave us one of the mate cabins to stay in as soon as we joined the pack. It's small and not updated, filled with only the bare essentials, but Addie is planning on continuing to live at the warehouse on her own until we've been together longer.

In the meantime, the guys and I already have plans to start building a bigger mate cabin to surprise her, for when she's ready to take this to the next level. For now, I'm just glad that we've finally found a good pack to join. We might not be their usual pack members, but they're good shifters, so they've accepted us. And every time I look over at my new mate and see the fire in her eyes, I'm thankful as hell that we found her.

What I'm *not* thankful for? The fact that Lafe decided he couldn't wait after all. Before I realize that his innocent nuzzling has changed, he's already unzipped his pants, pulled Addie onto his lap, and speared her with his cock.

"You motherfucker," I growl from the driver's seat.

"Duckerfucker, you mean," Lafe chuckles. His laugh cuts off onto a groan as he watches Addie bounce on top of him, her head tossed back with a moan.

When Herrick tries to climb into the backseat too, I punch him in the side of the head. "No, you don't. If I have to wait, you have to wait!" I bark.

Herrick just punches *me* in the arm, and then climbs to the backseat, anyway. *Asshole.*

I have to continue to drive and not get us into a wreck while listening to her moan and pant, which is basically fucking torture. I'm definitely making one of them drive next time, because this shit is *not* fair. When she screams out from an orgasm, I nearly run us off the road. My skin ripples with fur, my coyote baying inside of me.

Finally, we get to the compound and I floor it on our way to our cabin. When we get there, I throw the car into park and yank the keys out of the ignition, shoving them into my pocket. I get out and wrench open the back door. She's now riding on top of Herrick, her pale thighs wrapped around his dark ones, while Lafe fondles her tits. She's all flushed and perfect looking, and I can't take it anymore. I reach over, grip her by the waist and haul her off.

"What the fuck?" Herrick yells, but I don't care. Those assholes started without me, and now I'm gonna take my turn. I'm as hard as a fucking rock, and I can't wait. Not even the seconds it would take to carry her inside.

I pop open my pants, slam her against the side of the car, and plunge into her with one punishing thrust. She cries out a breathy, *"Yes,"* and now it's me that her legs are wrapping around. Herrick climbs out and pierces me with a glare. No regrets. The back of her head hits the window as I continue to plunge into her, and I see feathers popping up around her arms, but it only drives my lust crazier.

"Think you can fuck them while I'm stuck on the sidelines?" I growl into her ear. "I don't think so."

"So impatient," she retorts huskily.

I feel Herrick and Lafe approach on either side of me, so I pull out, drop her legs from around my waist, twist her around, and then bend her over. Herrick and Lafe each take one of her arms to hold while I slam into her from behind, and she screams in pleasure. "Fuck, yes!"

My pace is demanding and harsh. There is nothing tender about it, but I feel her pussy clenching around me as another orgasm approaches.

"You have two more mates," I remind her. "And remember? We don't like to wait turns."

In answer, Addie immediately reaches out to grip Herrick's dick while turning her head to take Lafe in her mouth. All four of us groan. "There you go," I ground out while I reach around to play with her clit. "There's our little mate, fucking all of us. Loving our cocks. I think she likes fucking all three of us at the same time."

"Fuck yes, she does," Herrick says. He reaches for her face and yanks her away from Lafe's dick, pulling her mouth toward his cock instead. She happily complies, instantly taking him in her mouth while reaching out to stroke Lafe.

Herrick fists a hand in her hair and thrusts into her, making her choke and moan. "That's it, swallow that cock," I tell her. "Good girl. You like being our dirty little shifter, don't you?"

My hand moves faster over her clit, and she screams around Herrick's dick as she explodes with pleasure. I feel her orgasm hit *hard*. Her pussy walls clench, making me blow my load deep inside of her, coating her insides. Herrick comes at the same time, and our good little mate swallows every drop of his cum before turning back to Lafe and sucking him off as well.

"Ducking hell," he hisses as she starts bobbing over him. "Just like that, babe. God, your mouth feels so good."

All she has to do is suck his balls into her mouth and jerk his dick in her hand, and then he's finishing, too.

When we're all done, panting and sticky, I smirk as Herrick swings her up into his arms and starts walking her into the house. She looks sexy as hell. Juices coating her thighs, hair mussed, clothes missing, our scent all over her, swollen lips, and best of all—a lazy, glazed look of pure satisfaction. It strokes my ego to know that *we* put that look on her face.

"Waddle we ever do without her?" Lafe smirks.

I roll my eyes at him as I start following behind Herrick into the cabin.

"Hey, how many coyotes does it take to make a duck show her O face?" Lafe calls out, jogging to catch up.

Addie laughs, and I swear the sound is sweeter than fucking music. "Three," she answers. "Now get your asses in the shower. I want round two in the water."

Yep. That's our mate, and she's perfect.

We have a long way to go to prove ourselves and deserve her, but I look forward to the challenge, and I know we'll be better for it. Hell, she's already made us better and happier, in the short amount of time we've known her. After years of wandering on our own, I'm grateful that we ended up here.

I guess three coyote preds just needed to find a duck to mate with and a pack of misfits to join to finally find our place in the world. Who knew?

The End. For now.

MORE MISFITS

Thank you for reading! I hope you loved the misfits as much as I do. I wanted to write a shifter series that featured unconventional animals who aren't so popular and are rarely, if ever, shown in shifter books. I also wanted to show that oddballs are cool too, and just because you're different, doesn't mean you aren't worthy.

I can't wait to show you what some of the other animals are in Pack Aberrant! Maybe you'll guess some of them with the little hints I've left...

This series will return with another misfit featured in the next book. Every book will be a standalone for that character, but will be a continuation of the Pack Aberrant story. Book one is a reverse harem with multiple love interests with the main character. However, this is not a reverse harem series. Some main characters in this series will have monogamous relationships.

ABOUT THE AUTHOR

Raven Kennedy lives in California with her family. She is most known for her international bestselling Heart Hassle series about a quirky cupid who wants to find love for herself. RK writes in a range of genres, including romantic comedies, dark romances, contemporary, paranormal, and fantasy. Whether she makes you laugh or cry, she hopes to connect with readers and create characters you can root for.

Printed in Great
Britain
by Amazon